Graffiti Hack

By Elen Ghulam

Graffiti Hack

ihath publishing

www.ihath.com

This is a work of fiction. While, as in all fiction, the literary perceptions and insights are based on experience. All names, characters, places and incidents are products of the author's imagination. No reference to any real person is intended or should be inferred.

ISBN 978-0978187217

For Rawan Hassan

To be or not to be?
That is a stupid question.

Prologue

Once upon a time, not so long ago and not that far away, lived a beautiful princess. This princess lived in a strange country, surrounded by mountains and filled with rivers and valleys. Everybody lived a peaceful and happy life. There were no recent memories of crimes or deprivations in these lands. On the contrary, love, beauty and polite manners were the mark of the citizens of this country. Then suddenly, one winter's night out of nowhere, a scary monster invaded the dreams of the fair princess. Every night, he repulsed the princess with his beastly appearance. He gnashed his teeth angrily, stomped his feet loudly and growled in hideous sounds that made even the tiniest of pomegranate pits shake in fear. He stole whatever he desired and killed whomever he wished, with nobody to defy him. The monster had declared itself the definitive master of the land.

Days and weeks passed, and the poor princess awakened every morning ravaged by her sleep. She hoped that someone would rescue her from this most disastrous affliction. Alas, all the brave heroes were in the land of sands battling a purple dragon with green teeth. After three weeks and two nights, the princess became petrified of sleep and decided to pursue a life with no rest—not even a wink. Weariness took its toll on the princess and within a month of the dreadful event, she became unable to work, move or think. Even when she sat still on a chair, she felt as if thousands of needles were poking her in every pore of her skin.

And so the princess languished in despair and sat in front of her laptop. She started to search on Google, hoping that she might find answers to her unique affliction. The princess searched the four corners of the Internet, but hours and hours of frantic searching yielded fifty-five questions and not a single solution. The precise moment of her deepest despair was when her iPod began to play a random shuffle song from the distant land of the dunes. The Phrygian tune, with its cycle of whole notes followed by semitones, opened a flood of yearning that couldn't be stopped. And that was when the princess realized that the Lord Almighty had no intention of sending a knight in shining armor, but would rather inspire that which was not planned. The princess felt a sudden tremor in her body, stopped the random clicking on her keyboard, and began to write a story.

Quari-ay-eh-ay

"I must learn to love and accept all people, even Americans."

I wrote in my diary on the first morning I spent in Washington, D.C. I had just left Quari-ay-eh-ay and had travelled a long distance to a strange land with a critical mission in mind.

Armed with my signature smile and a determined attitude, I believe I can achieve anything that I set my mind to. This time I aim high—I am about to embark on the most difficult task I have ever undertaken. This challenge will no doubt shape my character as much as I will shape it. As I embark upon my calling, I feel sweet pink tingles of anticipation roaming up and down my spine. How fantastic to know one's mission in life!

My name is Nelly Nasah. Before I tell you about what I am planning to do in Washington, D.C., let me first tell you a little about where I come from. I am the proud daughter of the magical kingdom of Quari-ay-eh-ay, which is not magical at all. It is called that because visitors experience a sense of awe upon seeing the intricate designs of the Quari-ay-eh-ayian architecture. In streets lined with pomegranate and fig trees, weeping fountains and breezy courtyards are the trademarks of each building. The busiest of businesses and the most austere of offices are built around a restful piazza with lush shrubs providing visual accompaniment to the sound of water trickling in the background. Each structure in my country is unique; in fact, we have strict bylaws forbidding imitation in new construction projects. Some are decorated with mosaics, others with large hand-painted tiles. Official buildings are supported with pink marble columns and are decorated with inlaid stucco lattice in geometric shapes. The wealthy like to build villas with ornate metalwork; the wealthiest use golden sheets instead. Many private residences have painted murals in different artistic styles. Despite the rich variety of designs, there is a strange, almost eerie sense of harmony in all the structures. It's something that befuddles scientists and artists alike—you have to see it with your own eyes in order to believe it. People give different explanations for the unusual magnificence in such non-uniformity—some attribute it to the evolved sense of aesthetics in the Quari people; others point to the plain and dreary landscape of the Quari land and explain that in a region of flat landscape, people need to create an alternate source of inspiration to that of nature. Whatever the reasons, there is no doubt about it—Quari-ay-eh-ay is a place dedicated to refined beauty in its most advanced form. It's in our blood. We are drawn to beauty, and simply can't help but to create it in everything upon which we fasten our gaze.

Visitors who stay longer than a couple of days realize that the evolved sense of ornamentals goes beyond buildings and permeates every aspect of Quari-ay-eh-ayian life.

Even food is presented in a decorative manner. Dishes are combined not just for their complimentary flavors and smells, but for harmony in color, as well. Rice is either colored with the lush orange of saffron or cooked with red peppers to give it pigment. Bread contains food coloring and is presented in purple, green or pink. Bits of carrot, shredded purple cabbage and chopped parsley are used to create elaborate mosaics on top of any dip, salad or casserole. A whole aisle is dedicated to cake sprinkles in any self-respecting supermarket. Cookie cutters and cake molds are a multimillion dollar industry in Quari-ay-eh-ay.

Clothing is another area where people exercise their decorative impulses. Although people purchase clothing from the same chain stores just like everybody else around the world, any self-identified Quari would burn with the fires of shame if seen wearing a white t-shirt and a pair of plain jeans—each one of us has our own individual method of embellishing our own attire. Embroidery, hand painting, silk screening, rhinestone gluing, iron-on transfers and tie-dyes are common methods used. You can easily tell the locals from tourists—only the tourists walk around in plain clothing. Even those tourists who try to fit in lack the refinement to create an elaborate design such as which comes naturally to us. An outsider attempting to conceal his outsideness creates a sloppy mess of colors that has neither rhyme nor logic, and he or she would be derided as an imposter. Non-locals are frequently advised to not attempt to imitate the Quari, for it takes a certain finesse and particular personality to carry off the Quari dedication to aesthetics. It's far better to be a plain tourist than a pretender clashing with the carefully constructed harmonious diversity of the Quari, offending the locals as you go along.

Language is an area of particular pride for the people of Quari-ay-eh-ay. The Quari use a cursive script, making each word a single complex stroke that morphs into a diagram. Quari can be written from right to left, left to right, bottom-up, diagonally, in a long spiral, or in whatever shape or direction the writer feels like. A page of text could easily take an anthropomorphic shape which depicts the emotion expressed in the text. A Quari typically starts writing by drawing out a diagram to get in touch with his emotions, and then continues by writing out his ideas along the lines of the diagram. Reading text in strict left-to-right straight lines seems wholly boring to the Quari people. Although familiar with computers and the Internet, the Quari prefer to ignore the medium until a more beautiful technology comes along—one which would enable us to be part of the World Wide Web revolution without offending our sense of harmony.

Everything in Quari-ay-eh-ay is decorated: The heart monitor machine in the intensive care unit, the common water fountain, the office desk, and even the humble wrist watch. It is theorized that the colorful designs of the Swatch® watches were inspired during the Swatch CEO's visit to Quari-ay-eh-ay. Upon seeing the colorful designs that Quari people created on their store-bought watches, the wildfire of inspiration seized him and he succumbed to the seduction of the Quari flare. Swatch Ltd. denies this origin of inspiration story. Luckily for them, we are a generous and hospitable bunch; we take joy in inspiring other nations and peoples towards beauty, even when it goes unacknowledged.

To visit Quari-ay-eh-ay is to have an explosion of your senses. Not only do your eyes get to feast, but your nostrils are invited to play, as well. The Quari people are fond of perfume, incense and essential oils. Quari-ay-eh-ay is not for the meek nose, nor the allergic temperament. If you cannot handle a cacophony of smells, you are well-advised to get out of the country. Rooms are infused with evaporated rose water, great halls with burning amber wood. Clothing is hung over burning essential oils to infuse them with the sweet smells of the orient. Each person announces his arrival first to your nose—even before your eyes—because the scents of their fragrances precede them. When a number of Quari are present in the same place, their collective perfumes blend together and bloom into a chemical reaction that creates a unique one-time sensory performance. Men and women alike smell beautiful. To shake the hand of a Quari means that your hand would carry the lingering fragrance of his or her perfume for days. The Quari are brilliant perfumers, and many of them know how to distill their own brew. In my country, nobody buys perfumes in a department store the way Americans do (although I must admit that Chanel No. 5 is agreeable to my sensibilities!). We prefer perfumes that hit your olfactory receptors with different notes over a rapid succession of time. O! A perfume should linger and hang in the air, don't you agree? The staying power of Quari perfumes makes dreams seem more real than reality. My friend Juliette, back home, is an expert perfumer. I buy the largest portion of my supply from her private cellar. Juliette will only sell you what is suitable for your personality and body chemistry. She is a strong believer in the aging process for essential oils. "Anything aged for fewer than 12 years is trash," Juliette is fond of saying in pontificating moments. Her perfume cellar is outfitted with shelves stretching floor to ceiling with color coded bottles of various liquids, waiting to be blended into one of her potent, yet delicate, creations. Juliette tells me that the perfume she mixes for me includes over 850 ingredients; it is a unique blend that represents my own personality. "Soft and intimate, a scent akin to a silk garment—so delicate, it feels like second skin," is how she describes it. "Violet leaves give the concoction a fresh, almost childlike quality, while sultry ylang-ylang, combined with spicy geranium, hints that this ethereal creation isn't all that innocent. Sophisticated, lighthearted and with hidden sensuality, a fragrance for intense moments"—just saying these words to you excites my nostrils. The inner lining of my nose is salivating with desire right this minute. I think the perfume Juliette makes for me has a bit of a soapy after-sniff, which I like—it hints at cleanliness and sharp endings. I would never dare tell Juliette that her perfume has an after-sniff, for fear that it would offend her. Who dares ruffle the feathers of her perfumer? .... Not I!

I, Nelly, am a true daughter of Quari-ay-eh-ay, through and through. I possess all the essential ingredients to be an ideal citizen of my home country. This is not a form of bragging, nor is it a case of misplaced pride. Allow me to illustrate with an example or two. Among my friends, I am famous for creating images inspired by the Sistine Chapel on top of baba ghanoush dishes. Using tiny shreds of cabbage, I recreate the pointing hand of God giving life to Adam. To add a bit of flair, I sprinkle little pieces of red pepper, drawing decorative flowerets. I am a fan of Michelangelo, for his technique was perfect. However, I feel that some of his creations were dreary and could be improved with a splash of color. Sometimes, for fun, I replace the hand of Adam with a feminine hand—imagining a scene where God creates Eve first. Drawing nail polish with paprika, a bracelet elegantly hanging off the wrist using cooked asparagus—the first woman comes to life through the direct touch of the divine. Such improvisations delight my friends when I present them at my neighborhood's monthly potluck brunch.

Between the edible sculptures, ice carvings, 3D fruit art and bread creations, my contributions never fail to make an impression. Although my dishes are flat—never 3D—my unique touch in decorating a humble hummus dish impresses the most refined of tastes. "You are an esthetician to be reckoned with!" my friend Juliette once told me. "Without you, our monthly potluck would not be the same," Ophelia would exclaim. Desdemona, typically composed and regal, once stepped outside her character and widened her eyes while examining one of my inspirations. "This is frightfully remarkable," she stated. I don't go through all this effort for accolades, but it does feel pleasant to be appreciated.

Perhaps I should tell you a little about my friends. There is Juliette, as I have already mentioned—she is the perfumer. Desdemona is the expert embroiderer in the group. She does crawling ivy decorations on trousers that will mesmerize you while you trace the branches and offshoots up a leg for hours. My favorite pair of jeans was decorated by Desdemona. It has a sparkly red design going down the right leg as if plucked from untamed wilderness. Whenever I wear those pants, I can feel Desdemona's passion seeping through the fabric into one leg and transferring to the other leg. The transference of energy from one side to the other makes me want to dance. Finally, there is Ophelia, o sweet, sweet Ophelia. She is the calligrapher and tea blender in the group. She can turn text into mesmerizing intricate shapes that will make you forget language. I met Desdemona and Juliette in high school, and we have remained friends since. Ophelia is the most recent addition to our group. She walked into the bookstore where I was working, and inquired about ideas for cake decoration. I showed her a few books and we began to talk. Three hours later, we realized that we were destined to be good friends. The four of us used to meet once a week on Thursdays at the Fruity Talk Café on the corner of Broadway and Columbia Street. They serve tarts decorated with fruit. My favorite is the coconut cream pie, which comes decorated with shreds of roasted coconut suspended in a thick, edible glaze—it makes the pastry look like a snow globe. Juliette likes to order berry pie decorated in flower shapes. Desdemona usually orders the banana chocolate cream pie that has intricate shapes drizzled in chocolate on top. Ophelia does not have a favorite; every week, she walks into Fruity Talk Café and contemplates all of the pies and tarts in the display, agonizing over her choice. We meet there regularly. We show each other our creative endeavors and brainstorm about how to make all aspects of our life more pleasing.

Although I am held in high regard by my dear friends, the person I crave to impress the most is my father's best friend, Sockless Miguel—or Uncle Miguel, as I call him. Uncle Miguel is a poet who speaks four languages. He has travelled all over the world and has actually seen the Sistine Chapel with his own eyes. He presides over the official cake decorations at the royal palace, and was instrumental in legislating the nonconformity laws in Quari-ay-eh-ay. Miguel is the crème de la crème of good taste.

Yet despite all his refinement, Uncle Miguel refuses to wear socks, opting instead to wear loafers on bare feet. His friends are always gifting him beautiful and uniquely designed socks in the hope that the right pair of socks might inspire him to change this habit. Some theorize that Miguel simply hasn't met a pair of socks that were up to his high standards; others rumor that he loves the feeling of leather against the soles of his feet, implying a more sinister reason for his sockless state. Miguel owns hundreds of pairs of socks which were all gifted to him on birthdays and other special occasions. Everybody who knows Uncle Miguel wants to win the honor of socking the sockless jewel of Quari-ay-eh-ay, yet his feet remain true to the nickname he carries—Sockless. As a child, I used to love going through Uncle Miguel's sock cabinet. Drawer upon drawer of mind boggling socks—embroidered, painted, fringed and ruffled. Some of his socks are made with such fine material, you would think they were sewn out of baby silk. Yet each pair sits there, waiting to fulfill its purpose: to cover feet. It must be a languished existence to be a sock in Uncle Miguel's drawer, each pair of socks taking turns lamenting with hungry anticipation.

I knew even then that if I could impress Uncle Miguel, I would go far in my life. I know I have his affection, but will I ever earn his respect?

Sigh! Only time will tell.

Mayonnaise

Food decoration is my specialty, but I dabble in embroidery, as well. I am not as good as Desdemona, but I manage just fine with creating designs on garments. My favorite is cross-stitch to create geometric shapes and floral patterns. My embroidered tablecloths and doilies are in demand as gifts. I have even discovered a way to cross-stitch the upholstery of my office chair with a tree of life motif. It took 48 hours of finger-numbing needlework to add birds, fruits and blossoms once the tree was finished. The end result was worth the effort. I wonder who is sitting in that chair right now? Whoever it is, I hope their life force is strengthened by their sitting in my chair.

In Quari-ay-eh-ay, I worked as a purchasing clerk in a bookstore called "Bookmark." It's a unique store—with each purchase, a client receives a one-of-a-kind handmade bookmark. All who work at the Bookmark Bookstore have to participate in bookmark making. It was my favorite part of the job. Instead of starting with a long strip of rectangular paper, I employed creativity in the shapes of bookmarks by cutting out a zigzag on one of the edges. I then proceeded by drawing intricate designs using felt pens. Over time, I developed a style all of my own. My distinctive form was inspired by the story of "The Rocks in a Mayonnaise Jar." My mother's boss told the story at her funeral.

It was the most touching speech given on that sad day; his eulogy stuck with me like a clingy wet cotton dress.

Let me tell you the story of the rocks in the mayonnaise jar. I know I am digressing, and I do feel eager to get back to Washington, D.C., as well. However, if you invest a few extra minutes, your patience shall reap the rewards of a mighty gem of a story:

A wise philosophy professor met with his students in a university auditorium. This professor had been lecturing for 20 years, yet he never tired of teaching this one particular lesson. He stood in front of his students in silence, waiting patiently for all to settle into their seats. When he sensed that he had everyone's attention, he picked up a large, empty and a clean mayonnaise jar from beneath his desk, and proceeded to fill it to the top with rocks about two inches in diameter. With a confident look and a knowing smile, he said, "Raise your hand if you think this jar is full". His voice travelled all the way to the last row; the auditorium vibrated with his presence. The students all agreed that the jar was full. So, the professor picked up a box of small pebbles that were hidden under the desk, and he poured them into the jar. He shook the jar gently. The pebbles rolled into the empty spaces between the larger rocks. He then asked the students again whether the jar was full. All answered in unison that it was, indeed, full.

The professor next picked up a box of sand and poured it into the jar. The sound of the sand rustling against stone filled the room while the sand flowed into the remaining spaces between the pebbles and the rocks.

"Now, " said the professor, raising his voice to a higher pitch, "I want you to contemplate this full mayonnaise jar as if it were your life. The rocks are the most important things—your family, your partner, your health, your children (when and if you have them one day)—things that, if everything else were lost and only they remained, your life would be full. The pebbles are the other things that matter, like your career, your home and your passions. The sand is everything else—the small stuff, paying bills, entertainment, keeping the kitchen cupboard organized.

"If you put the sand into the jar first, there will be no room for the pebbles and the rocks. The same goes for your life—if you spend all your time and energy on getting the car fixed or observing the lives of others, you will never have room for the things that are important to you.

"Pay attention to the things that are critical to your happiness. Play with children. Spend time with your partner. There will always be time to go to the mall, clean the house, give a dinner party or wash the carpet.

"Take care of the rocks first—the things that are of the upmost importance. Set your priorities. The rest is just sand."

The professor paused. This is when he typically searched his students' eyes for a moment of recognition. He savoured seeing the aha! percolate through the malleable minds of the young and restless. Every year, one or two students walked out of the auditorium transformed by the lesson. It gave the professor a powerful motivation to continue teaching.

This time, however, something new happened—something unexpected.

A student stood up and in a slow pace, walked up to the professor's desk. He took the jar, which the other students and the professor had agreed was full, and proceeded to pour into it a cup of coffee.

The coffee flowed into the remaining spaces within the container, making swooshy sounds as the liquid made the jar pregnant with fullness.

"See!" the cheeky student said, beaming with delight. "The moral of this tale is, no matter how full your life is, there is always room for sharing a cup of coffee with a friend."

The auditorium burst into a rapture of delight. Some cheered, others clapped; the most brazen hooted.

On that day, it was the professor's turn to do the learning.

At my mother's funeral, my mother's boss said that my mother exemplified this story. "She always knew what her priorities were, never missing one day of work in 15 years—not even when she was sick. Yet her life was full with a marriage, a child and a rich social life."

My bookmark drawings always started with an outline of a few shapes, and then I filled each shape with smaller shapes that resembled rocks. Picking up a different color, I drew even smaller shapes—like the pebbles—and finally, using a fourth color, I drew dots to symbolize the sand in the story. The mixture of shapes and colors created an enticing mixture that bookmark customers began to call "Nelly's design," but I liked to call it the "mayonnaise jar design." Oh, how I enjoy telling the story of the rocks in a mayonnaise jar...I will never tire of telling it.

In addition to making bookmarks, I enjoyed other aspects of my job back home. It was the perfect occupation for me at the time. I spent my workdays exploring new books from around the world, thinking about which particular ones would most inspire the clients of Bookmark Bookstore. Working there was free education for me—I was privy to all the knowledge that was tucked away in the thousands of books stocked by Bookmark. I loved meeting new people at the bookstore, helping them select the perfect reading companion. The only part I didn't enjoy about my employment there was having to use the computer to fill out purchase orders.

Overtime, I had to use the computer more and more, as publishing houses were issuing their catalogues digitally. Fingering through a catalogue, filling out paper forms with a pen and unwrapping packages are sensual delights. In contrast, typing on a keyboard, reading uniformly straight lines and staring at a flat monitor for hours on end seemed to me a poor relative of the non-digital equivalent of these activities. My boss, Mr. Trevrel—the owner of Bookmark Bookstore—insisted the digital age was upon us, and we had to embrace it. "Doing these tasks on a computer is more efficient," he would state in his whispery hoarse voice. I deployed different tactics to persuade Mr. Trevrel to change his mind. "The computer produces a low-level humming sound which is disturbing the bookstore's fine ambience," was one of my many arguments. "How do we encourage our customers to purchase books when they see us staring at monitors?" was yet another. Mr. Trevrel would invite me to sit down in his office, and would listen to my complaints attentively, shaking his head as if he were approving. Then, after inquiring as to whether I were finished with my side of the story, he would spend an hour or more slowly and tediously expounding upon the revolutionary benefits of using a computer. Arguing with Mr. Trevrel was never fun. He wouldn't dismiss me outright, but rather listened courteously to every word I said and then forced me to listen to him at great length. He is a 76-year-old man who embodies gentlemanly qualities from a bygone era—always polite, always soft-spoken. He is the only man I know who has an infatuation with Mother Teresa—a photo of her is displayed on his desk in his tiny office. He frequently repeats quotes he attributed to her: "Words which do not give the light of love increase the darkness" "Be faithful in small things because it is in them your strength lies." A paradox of a man. He is suspended between two ideals—that of a saint, and the father of modernity. I wonder whether Mother Teresa approved of the digital age, and if she would have been able to dissuade Mr. Trevrel to change his mind. Instead of dismissing me with a hand wave while commanding me to do as I was told, he felt always compelled to discuss it with me until I was too tired of talking about it. I would rather pretend that I was agreeing with him than prolong my ordeal; relenting was easier than listening to hours of his rational arguments, which were punctuated with stories from his childhood. The childhood of his seven children would then follow. And tall tales of his two marriages were a staple at the store.

I delighted myself by drinking floral tea while working the machine. My logic was, "If my eyesight and fingers had to be subjected to a dreary activity, my taste buds and nostrils should at least be having a fiesta." My favorite is a mix of rosebuds, vanilla, coconut shreds and jasmine infused with a touch of lavender. This particular mixture was the creation of dear Ophelia. Her objective in life was to create the ultimate tea blend, and she was therefore constantly experimenting, using her friends as taste testers. I enjoyed most of her flower-based blends, and would always write down a detailed review for her reference. It gives me great pleasure to be able to help people in their creative endeavors. Ophelia has varied theories about tea; she believes that there are three essential cups of tea which a person must drink during each day.

"The first cup of tea must be bitter, to be drunk first thing in the morning in order to remind oneself of the bitterness of life. The bitterness helps the person wake up, facing the day with the right perspective. The second cup of tea is to be consumed mid-day and must be sweet to remind oneself of the necessity of enjoying life despite hardships. The third cup of tea is to be consumed before going to bed, and must be light like the silent breath of death."

Ophelia also believes that tea must be drunk in solitude, because the delicate flavors require mindful contemplation. Coffee, however, in her book, is for social gathering, because the bold flavor does not require the same attention. I sensed that Ophelia was offended whenever one of us ordered a cup of tea at our Fruity Talk gatherings, because it broke one or more of her rules about proper tea consumption. I, myself, found her rules interesting, but did not follow them religiously. Flaunting my digressions would have been disrespectful, and so I opted to avoid entirely drinking tea in her presence.

The Nightmare

It started out as a day like any other in a long string of days that had marked my existence. I wish I could tell you it was a stormy morning, that the wind howled and the trees swayed from side to side, performing a dance to the howling music of moving air. I wish I could tell you that I woke up that morning with a premonition of upheavals about to seize my existence. It would make for a more mysterious story. It would also mark me as a liar. The boring truth is, I remember nothing at all about the weather or my inner state until the point at which I sat down at my desk at work to fill out an invoice. I clicked on the wrong icon and found myself staring at a box with a search button next to it on the screen. Without knowing why, a brief impulse seized my fingers. I typed "Socks for Miguel" and clicked the search button. A slew of text appeared before my eyes, lines organized into formations like an army brigade. Each time I clicked on one, more appeared, spawning like frogs. Mindlessly, I became absorbed in clicking on random links, hopping from one website to another until I reached a website called "GypsyRumor.com". Appalled was the state I was in for a long time afterwards. I sensed a wobbling in both my knees; a slight constriction came over my breathing. I found myself involuntarily holding my breath in my lungs, forgetting to breathe out. Suffering from this first episode of apnea, I had to keep reminding myself to exhale, lest I would lose consciousness. The website was atrociously designed; in fact, most of the websites I accidently visited were poorly designed, yet GypsyRumor.com stopped me in my clicking tracks. It employed purple and green as its major color theme. There is nothing wrong with mixing these colors together, as long as the shades are right, but this was orchid purple with teal green, which everybody knows don't go together. To add to the disgrace, the website featured graphics of squirrely shapes that gave me a woozy feeling. There was a mixture of fonts of all different types, which must have given any reader a headache. In despair, I shut down my computer and walked away in disgust.

That night bore no shade of resemblance to the morning that had preceded it. I lay in bed in my room which I decorated around the red sheer curtains I had hand-embroidered with golden thread to resemble climbing ivy. Everything in my room followed the same motif (rooted in the ground, yet yearning towards the sky). This was the place where I felt most safe, yet all I could think about was the ugliness I had witnessed earlier in the day. Each time I closed my eyes, I would see text in Helvetica alternating with text in Times New Roman. I opened my eyes in horror. I tried to focus my vision on the carefully arranged flower bouquet standing on the side table next to my bed, in an attempt to filter the disturbing image out of my head. As my eyes began to close again, I saw orchid purple alongside teal green. I looked at the bedside table which I hand-painted myself, depicting soil at the bottom, grass in the mid-section and a sky full of fluffy clouds at the top. No matter how beautiful the object I fixated my gaze upon, disturbing visuals flooded my consciousness, waves chased by bigger waves. All night, I swung between states of sleep and wakefulness, a perpetual pendulum fueled by gravitational pull beyond understanding.

The next morning, I went to work feeling like I had been drowning in a swimming pool all night, barely gasping enough air for survival. Exhausted and weak from the lack of sleep, I lifted my spirits by leafing through beautiful books on house decoration. I then moved on to the cake decoration sections, and began to read a book on cupcake icing. Seeing images of smooth icing piped carefully on top of baked dough comforted my soul. I started to feel like myself again. Spending the rest of my day in my usual routine, I vowed never to surf the Internet and never, ever to click on random links, for such idle pursuits have unpredictable outcomes.

The next night, I went to bed with thoughts of my new design for next month's neighborhood potluck brunch. I was planning to create a quiche decorated with savory icing which looked like a giant cupcake. My plan was to shred tomatoes and cucumbers to look like cake sprinkles. The savory impersonating the sweet carries deep symbolism. I am certain that I don't need to explain this to you. I closed my eyes, contemplating this new culinary challenge, hoping for dreams of eggyana— a land where eggs are on top of the food chain and omelets are made using dead chicken carcasses. Little did I know, destiny was having a laughing fit at the modesty of my yearnings.

I had a nightmare instead. A white snake the size of a giant slithered into my dream life. Shining with grey and green hues when encountering a ray of sunlight, this horrifying beast dazzled with a flicker of beauty. Tangled up in several knots, one on top of the other, the snake looked like a four-story building that might crumble with the right seismic activity. I became overwhelmed with the sense that the very minute the snake became untangled, danger would ensue. I awoke in horror with a feeling of menace hanging over my head. My back muscles where aching, especially on the left side. I also felt tension in my lower jaw. Night after night the same nightmare recurred, except that each night, there were more details. The snake bared its teeth at me and made hissing sounds that paralyzed me with fear. In the dream, I saw myself standing still in front of the snake. I stood there, watching, unable to take defensive action. I awakened every morning weary with restlessness. A sense of doom dominated my thoughts all day long. I tried reading poetry before going to sleep, reading stories about fairies and drawing pictures of peacocks frolicking in a garden, but no amount of positive thinking pushed the white monster out of my dreams. I devised a set of stretching exercises to relieve the aches in my back and jaw—I must have been clenching my mouth while I slept. After 20 nights of twisting and turning in bed, I decided that the only way to kick this horror out of my existence would be to avoid sleep altogether. Every night, I made myself a cup of Turkish coffee and occupied myself with reading until dawn. This lack of sleep began to impact my mental abilities. I wasn't able to focus at work. All I could come up with for the monthly potluck dish was a smiley face drawn using store-bought icing on top of plain cupcakes. As a result of my constant state of tiredness, I accidentally applied the icing on top of my freshly baked cupcakes while they were still hot. The smiley faces melted and looked more like frowny faces by the time they were presented at the communal serving table. My friends Juliette, Ophelia and Desdemona looked at the cupcakes with concern and didn't say very much. Uncle Miguel took a single glance at my newest creation and asked me, with worry in his baritone voice, "Are you alright, my dear?"

I had hit rock bottom. It was one thing to bungle things at work and fill out invoices in place of purchase orders, but to not earn a single compliment at the neighborhood potluck was an absolutely new low. I knew I had to do something drastic to shake myself out of this state. I combed the books at Bookmark Bookstore, searching for a remedy for nightmares. Hours of reading didn't yield much. Finally the thought popped into my head—why not click the Internet icon on my computer and search for a remedy for nightmares? My previous encounter with the Internet had been scary enough and I wasn't sure I wanted to repeat the exercise. In fact, I suspected that my predicament was mysteriously related to my earlier Internet misadventure. "Cure me with that which was my disease", I remembered the old Quari proverb saying. If somehow I had caught my ailment from the Internet, perhaps I could find a cure from the same source, I reasoned in my sleep-deprived state.

Reluctantly, I sat at my computer, too tired to prepare my customary computer usage cup of tea. I clicked on the same Internet icon and typed, "The meaning of white snake in a dream," and hit the return button, holding my breath. Yet again, I had to remind myself to exhale in order to not faint. A group of links materialized on the screen. Closing my eyes, I took a deep breath and prayed that I would be guided to click on the right links and steered away from atrociously designed websites. "O God!" I called out in desperation. "I can handle plainness, I can take the lack of good taste, and I can even accept unrefined designed which are works-in-progress. But please spare my eyes the sights of ugliness that terrorize my sleep!" I opened my eyes, exhaled, and proceeded to surf the Internet gingerly.

The first website I visited was plainly designed with a matching hue of green and blue. "Not too bad," I puffed out in relief. The website stated:

"To see a snake or be bitten by one in your dream signifies hidden fears and worries that are threatening you. Your dream may be alerting you to something in your waking life that you are not aware of or that has not yet surfaced. The snake may also be seen as phallic and thus symbolize dangerous and forbidden sexuality. The snake may also refer to a person around you who is callous, ruthless, and can't be trusted. As a positive symbol, snakes represent transformation, knowledge and wisdom. It is indicative of self-renewal and positive changes."

The second link that I clicked on brought up a website designed in two columns, one wide and the other narrow. The top of the home page was decorated with a banner that had green and yellow geometric shapes. The website was simple, yet elegant. "So far, so good," I thought to myself. On this second website, a woman was describing her dream:

"Does anybody know how to interpret dreams? I had a vivid dream last night. My husband, my son and I were carrying a huge white python. We were carrying it for a long time while walking around town, the beach and city center. Finally we got home and placed the white python in our bath tub.

Any clues what that means?"

There were many responses to the question, each with a different interpretation. Some said that the snake symbolizes an enemy; others said that it meant evil; yet others prophesied visions of holiness. The most interesting response stated:

"Well! white is a good thing, it means innocence. Walking around the city is like you are trying to show the people of the city what to do and what you have found. Now the snake itself may refer to two things:

1) either the snake refers to the original sin. If this is the case you will probably commit to something that will remove all sinfulness that might cloud your life.

2) that is one meaning, so if the snake refers to danger or an enemy that you will be able to get rid of.

The only thing that I do not like is the bathtub in the dream.... if you saw it as part of the whole bathroom that's not a good thing because it's a reference to filthiness. if you saw just the bathtub then maybe your whole dream is not bad after all, 'cause it may just mean cleanliness."

The third attempt brought a website that had no graphics at all—it was text only. It had a solid blue line across the top. The text was in simple black. I was grateful for its plainness, since I knew of the horrific alternatives that had previously assailed me. This website stated:

"Snakes represent enemies and the things you fear in real life. When you dream about snakes, be more cautious in the waking hours. It is a foreboding feeling that a bad turn of events can happen suddenly as a snake would strike rapidly on its unsuspecting prey. You will feel betrayal from people you least expect."

Given all the good fortune that I had encountered with my clicking, I decided to not push my luck, and turned off my computer. I placed the palms of my hands towards the sky to show gratitude: "Thank you, God, for steering me away from hideously designed websites that assault my senses," I whispered quietly under my breath. I decided to take all the information I had learned and think about it at home. I was certain that if I thought deeply about it, I would come up with the correct dream interpretation for myself. A remedy to my sleepless state was now within reach.

That night, I went home and sat down at my desk with a notebook and pen. I drew an outline of a large entangled snake and began to write all possible interpretations of my dream: "Envy, enemy ... perhaps there is an enemy in my life who is envious of me. I need to take that enemy to the bathtub and clean them of their sins. Hidden fears—what are my hidden fears? I have a phobia of badly designed anything—Like that poorly designed website I had seen. In fact, I think my nightmare came from seeing it. I must confront my fears and challenge them. I need to be proactive and correct the wrongs that I see. In the dream, I am passive. The dream is telling me to be active. Active means taking charge of things...."

I wrote a stream of consciousness into the dawn, hoping to arrive at the root cause of my predicament. In the morning, I realized that I had actually fallen asleep for the first time in a month. Face down on top of my notebook, I felt a sense of exhilaration at having slept a few winks of restful sleep. In that moment, I looked down and saw in big letters, right in the middle of the snake shape, "Take Control of Your Ailment". An idea popped into my head and I knew exactly what I needed to do: I would travel to Washington, D.C—to the capital city of the country, where the Internet had been invented, and liberate the world of badly designed websites. If people had elegantly designed web pages, this would inspire them to create beauty in every other aspect of their lives. I had a sense of the purpose of my life. The details were fuzzy, but I knew what I needed to achieve. Disambiguating the riddle of my nightmare left me with a sense of tired relief, like a knight in shining armor returning to his princess after slaying a multi-headed dragon. My muscles ached in my shoulders and chest. I was stinky with sweat. A headache of excess concentration was knocking on the door of my awareness. Yet I sensed a faint happiness emerging from the left side of my waist. A few warm drops of honey were melting, creating the potential to mix with my blood, spreading sweetness to the rest of my body over time. This virtual world on the Internet was merely a reflection of the inner world of these web designers, who themselves reflect the societies in which they were raised. "Curing the symptom would cure the disease", I reasoned in my newfound alleviated state. This challenge had been placed in my path by destiny, and within it laid the secret to unlocking my appointed quest.

Shoes

I gathered my closest friends, Juliette, Ophelia and Desdemona, to announce my imminent departure. In my living room, I served blueberry scones, tea and pomegranate juice to accompany the announcement of my upcoming trip to the U.S.

Juliette passionately said, "But things will only improve in Quari-ay-eh-ay. What will you do in the U.S.? You will be bored there. Think of all the plain buildings, plain food and plain clothing."

Ophelia added, skeptically, "Many Quari people in the past have tried to teach foreigners good taste before you, and failed miserably. Consult with Sockless Miguel. He has travelled all over the world. Ask him if he managed to convert a single foreigner into understanding discrimination. What makes you think that you will succeed where others have failed? What makes you so special?"

Desdemona was the most cheerful about my news. "This is the craziest idea I have ever heard. I love it and hate it. Please write to us as frequently as possible and tell us all about your adventures".

I purchased a ticket to Washington, D.C., and booked a room at the Carlyle Hotel near DuPont circle—a large roundabout that has the whole city revolving around it the way the sun demanded that planets submit to its gravitational pull. Packing my luggage was an ordeal. I had never travelled anywhere, and was clueless as to what I might need in a foreign country. I didn't have much of a plan, but reasoned that I would show up and figure things out as I went along. On the day of my departure, Uncle Miguel brought his minivan to help transport my eight suitcases to the airport. My friends gathered around to say their final goodbyes. Juliette gave me a pink alarm clock decorated with white and purple rhinestones. "You will need this to keep you on time over there. Everything runs by the clock in the foreign lands," she told me while holding back tears. Desdemona gave me a charm bracelet with hanging hearts. "Wear this to remind you of the people back home who love you". Ophelia presented me with a single peacock feather, declaring, "I read in a novel called *The Joy Luck Club* how a woman gave her daughter a swan's feather, telling her, 'This feather may look worthless, but it comes from afar and carries with it all my good intentions.' That line stuck with me and I've always fantasized about using it in real life. I didn't expect that my chance would come so soon. But a peacock's feather is much more beautiful. This feather is a symbol of all that we hold dear. It comes from Quari-ay-eh-ay, and carries with it all my prayers for you."

I was choking back saliva, which generates in excess when I am faced with awkward social situations. My stomach was grumbling and the bottoms of my feet felt itchy. To everybody around me, I looked perfectly composed. This was my vice—hiding my feelings. I could muster a poker face even in the most stressful of situations. Over the years, I had developed the reputation of being a tough woman. "More manly than men, stronger than a horse" was some of what was said about me. I said my goodbyes, kissed and hugged everybody and got into

Uncle Miguel's minivan, resisting the urge to look back at the goodbye party waving at me as the vehicle moved away. Ophelia poured a bowl of water on the back of the minivan as we drove away. Such was the custom in Quari-ay-eh-ay—thrown water was thought to shower blessings on a travelling person. I was grateful that the water wasn't poured over my head. At the airport, I gave Uncle Miguel a heartfelt hug and thanked him for his help. Sockless Miguel looked at me with sorrow in his eyes and said, "Remember that you are going to a foreign land with foreign customs. Over there, you are the foreigner and they are the locals. Try to blend in, and your experience will be more pleasant."

His parting words surprised me, for I was going there to serve others. "Blending in" helps nobody and one makes no difference. But I didn't argue with Uncle Miguel, attributing his strange parting advice to stress from his job.

At last, I was inside an airplane. I felt a strange mixture of heartache and exhilaration. Here I was, embarking on an adventure the likes of which nobody had yet to attempt. On the other hand, I was giving up the company of everybody I loved and everything that was familiar. I tried to distract myself from all the busy thoughts racing in my head by reading a magazine I found inserted in the pocket of the seat in front of me. In it, I read an interesting story that went like this (this isn't the way the article was written in the magazine, but rather the way I would recount it later in my diary):

There once was a girl named Tania Tulip, whose parents had fled a war-torn country in search of a better future for their children. Once in America, her father told her, "Study hard, my daughter, get good grades in school, and you will go far in this life". Tania studied hard every night and got good grades. Her father was pleased with her. The look of pride in her father's eyes filled Tania's heart with happiness and made everything in her life seem right. When Tania finished the seventh grade, her marks were the highest among all her classmates. Tania was selected to give a speech in front of her entire school. For two weeks, Tania was cooped up in her room, thinking about what to write. Whenever her father asked her about the speech, she told him that it was a surprise. When the seventh grade graduation came, Tania stood up proudly at the podium and delivered the following speech:

"Hello! My name is number 100428 and I am an alien from planet Slinkomaki". The crowd began to laugh. "When I landed here seven years ago, everything seemed strange. For example, the way the doors in the school need to be opened by hand when motion sensor technology is available on your planet. Or the way humanoid children run around in random directions during recess when transport in orderly straight lines is more efficient. I used to sit on a bench in the playground and wonder what children were doing at what you call 'monkey bars'. What is the purpose of climbing those things back and forth, back and forth, day after day? However, my teacher welcomed me and gave me a warm reception. Whenever I felt confused, she kindly pointed out the right direction. Over the years, I have grown to like your planet and enjoy its many beauties. If one day a humanoid chooses to visit planet Slinkomaki, I will do my utmost to return the courtesy. I still don't understand the meaning of monkey bars, nor the logic of moving in inefficient curves and wasting energy skipping around, but I do know that I will miss this school when I go to high school."

The crowd cheered, laughed and howled at Tania's speech. Parents walked up to Mr. and Mrs. Tulip, and congratulated them on the brilliant speech their daughter had just given. Tania's father was beaming with pride, so moved was he by the speech that he gave his daughter a lengthy hug and told her that he would buy her anything her heart desired.

Without thinking, Tania asked for a pair of red waterproof boots she had seen in a store. All summer long, Tania wore her new boots, went skipping to the park in them, and took great joy in jumping into puddles and kicking little rocks.

When Tania finished high school, her grades were sky-high. Her father advised her to consider enrolling in medical school. Tania studied even harder, and when it came time to choose a specialization, she fell in love with podiatric surgery. With a knife and a scalpel, Tania learned to fix bunions, bone fractures and deformed toes. Right after her shift was over in the hospital, she would run to the nearby shopping mall and browse the shoe stores. Tania owned 40 pairs of shoes in all the different colors of the rainbow. She was always on the lookout for yet another unique pair to add to her collection. However, because her job required hours of standing on her feet, most of her shoes proved uncomfortable for her daily routine. Tania spent countless hours of her free time improving her shoes. She would alter straps and add cushioning in an effort to create a pair of shoes that were both comfortable and stylish. All of her co-workers wore runners to work, but they looked unfashionable. Tania preferred to damage her feet than wear ugly shoes.

One day, Tania went home after a long workday feeling tired. Her feet were aching and she had a headache. The next day she didn't feel much better, but she decided to go to work, anyway. She tried to perform all the scheduled surgeries as usual. At the end of the day, she was called into the department head's office and was informed that she had committed a huge error. She had reattached a severed left toe to the right foot, and now the patient had two toes on the same foot. She was instructed to take a leave of absence until the legal mess was over.

Tania was devastated. She spent the first two weeks crying in her bed, and then it took her three weeks just to work up the courage to inform her family what had happened. For the first time since Tania could recall, she had nothing to do to fill her days. There was no work, no studying and no structure to her days. Even her weekly visit to the shopping mall became boring, because why would you buy shoes when you have no job to wear them to? To give herself structure, Tania forced herself to take long walks in the forest trails right behind her house. She would take slow, steady steps and attempt to contemplate what had gone wrong with her life. Tania had never felt so miserable in her whole existence; she was a disappointment to everybody around her.

One day during her daily walk, she encountered a puddle along the trail and remembered the summer she'd spent wearing red boots, jumping into puddles. She remembered all the happiness she had felt during that magical time. She remembered that, in fact, she had never felt so happy ever since. A tingly feeling came over her entire body, and she rushed home and sat at a note pad. Tania began to design her ideal shoe. It was red, waterproof, incredibly comfortable, and stylish. Three weeks later, Tania resigned her job as a podiatric surgeon and began her work on her Puddle Jumper shoe company. Her shoes were a huge hit all over the world. What she had attempted to achieve with a scalpel, she could now give to the world though her unique designs. Tania then met the man of her dreams and lived happily ever after wearing nothing but beautiful comfortable shoes.

I put the magazine back into the pocket of the seat in front of me, thinking it was the perfect story to have read at the beginning of my journey. It filled my heart with contentment where weariness had resided a few minutes earlier. Even the itching in my feet was gone. "Encountering this story is an omen," I told myself. "Tania's story is an allegory for the story I am about to live." After that, I fell asleep and slept all the way to Washington, D.C.

Elvi

"The bitter sand of foreignness," a common expression in Quari-ay-eh-ay, refers to a particular sentiment Quari people feel when they dwell abroad for periods longer than three weeks. It summons the visual of a person tasting sand, an awful predicament at the best of times. When that sand is not even the soil of your own dear motherland, that is when your taste buds open up to the full tang of the bitterness. It's an expression I've heard many times in the past in stories, poems and daily conversations. Now that I have lived in Washington, D.C., for three months, I find myself reflecting on it deeply. I am imagining myself with a mouthful of dirt right now. I am missing even the things that I hated about Quari-ay-eh-ay, like breakfast. Waking up in the morning with the thought of decorating food would cause me to imagine handcuffs restraining me to my bed's wooden headboard, rendering me incapable of leaving the bed for the rest of the day. Who wants to decorate oatmeal when you are still half-asleep and would rather just eat a banana and get out of the house? Or those trivial local sitcoms that are aired every June, which have no plot, yet contain excessive drama. I suspect that I am the only person in Quari-ay-eh-ay who doesn't appreciate them; everybody else talks about the latest episode of "The Running of the Horses, Like the Flowing of the River" or "The Mysterious Happenings of Mischief in Far and Outlands of

Habel". I am even missing hearing people discuss that horrid animated cartoon called "The Dreams and Aspirations of the Eggplant-Hating Peacock". I never thought I would miss looking at a flat horizon, the communal morning sing-alongs or hair decoration day. Yet here I am, sensing hollowness in my bones for things I used to complain about.

The first few weeks in Washington were exhilarating. I explored the city, sampled new food and spent hours in coffee shops, observing the behavior of Washingtonians, eavesdropping on their conversations, hoping to learn as much as possible about their culture. In my third week, I rented an apartment on 23rd and G Streets, in a neighborhood called "Foggy Bottom." I guess that whoever built the city was too lazy to come up with names for streets, and so decided to stick with sequential numbers and letters ... how dull can a city engineer be? My apartment building is plain white, and I prefer it that way. I knew I could always decorate the inside of my one-bedroom apartment in a fashion that would cozy me up. By week four, I had secured a job in a graphic design/software development company as a graphic designer. I assembled a colorful portfolio of elaborate designs; the artistic director at Snugoo.com hired me without enquiring about my education or experience. At that point, I felt optimistic that I was on my way to accomplishing my ambitious goal of reforming the Internet. I wanted to create designs of great beauty and elegance while working for the clients of Snugoo.com—my designs would elevate the sensitivity of each and every website owner. Even the puniest of puny websites, even personal blogs would be pleasant to view ... one day. In the meantime, I busied myself learning the ropes of my new trade as a junior graphic designer at Snugoo.com.

I am now, for the first time, feeling grateful to my former boss in Quari-ay-eh-ay, Mr. Trevrel, who forced me to use the computer, getting me to develop rudimentary computer skills which are now proving quite handy in my current job. "All the hard times I gave that poor Mr. Trevrel", I think to myself whenever I start up my computer in the morning. "I argued with him for hours about not using the computer, and look at me now—I depend on it!" I chuckle at my own stubbornness.

Snugoo.com's offices are located on the fourth floor of a five-story building built in 1895. It was originally intended to be a warehouse for a trading company, and later, in the 60's, was refurbished and converted to an office building. The building is characterized by its round-arched windows, brick façades and rough-dressed sandstone. The highlights of the building are eight large stone rosettes decorating the street façade. Snugoo is located in the upscale Georgetown neighborhood, yet had you seen the vicinity, you would have suspected it was located in a backwater decrepit area. A few minutes' walking distance from elegant shops and restaurants, a staircase cuts away from tourist funk into a giant ditch that has a river streaming through it. The ditch in question is called the "Chesapeake and Ohio Canal," a reddish dirt path dots by brick buildings that match the ambience. The locale of my employment has lots of character and personality, but my favorite is the elevator. It's a rickety old elevator that sways from side to side every time it moves. I like the wooden panel walls with little nightstand-style light fixtures on each wall. It has thick brass handles installed across three sides, as if the designer were expecting that you'd want to hold on to something while riding in this elevator. Was somebody dreaming of a launch into outer space? When I am by myself in the elevator, I imagine that I am in a dance school, the shiny brass doors doubling as a mirror. I hold onto one of the handles and pretend I am in a ballet class practicing pliés. The ceiling of the elevator is lined with backlit colored stained glass featuring an elaborate rose design. Over time, I came to appreciate my daily rides in the elevator. I call him Elvi—short for Elevator. Whenever I enter the elevator on my own with nobody around, I greet him by saying, "Good morning, Elvi, how are you today?" I half expect to hear a response one day; instead, Elvi sways happily from side to side.

Ashley

My interaction with my co-workers at Snugoo is less jovial. I sit at a metal desk behind Ashley, a middle-aged, talkative man. He tells tall tales—I never know whether they are real or not. When I first met Ashley, I was forced to suppress a giggle by turning it into a sneeze. Ashley is a woman's name in Quari-ay-eh-ay. He reminds me of the lyrics to the Johnny Cash song, "A Boy Named Sue". The song tells the outlandish yet heartfelt tale of a young man's desire for revenge on an absent father, who failed in his lone parental contribution to Sue's life by giving him a gender-inappropriate name. Ridicule and bullying followed the boy as he grew into a young man. A chance encounter with the father turned into a vicious brawl. After the two had beaten each other nearly senseless, Sue's father declared that the name was given as an act of love—Sue's father had given him that name to make sure that he grew up strong, to compensate for the absence of parental guidance. Learning this, Sue forgave his father, and they had an emotional reconciliation. Sue came to realize that his tough demeanor was the result of confronting so much teasing from a young age. The moral of the story is, "What ails you blesses you." I do hope that Ashley is blessed in some mysterious way by all that ails him. Unfortunately, no evidence of such grace has been detected by my senses.

"Good Morning," I greet Ashley while passing him in the morning, and true to his character, he responds by saying, "What is so good about it?" Most people just ignore Ashley and walk by him, but I find it necessary to respond to his question by listing a few examples. "The way the birds were singing this morning" or "The fact that we are alive" or "I love the way my coffee tastes in the morning." Ashley responds by telling me a tale of doom and gloom from his life, intended to add a faltering quiver to my positive perspective.

Every day there is a new story from Ashley; had he been a slightly more credible person, his stories would break your heart. Today's story went something like this:

"I used to be a dashing man. I know you find this hard to believe, but I exercised regularly in the gym, had a fantastic six-pack and all my teeth. When my wife kicked me out of the house, she threw my clothes and all my belongings in the front yard and left them there for two whole days while it rained. Before I had a chance to collect my stuff, everything got soaked. All my suits, Versace shoes and silk shirts were ruined. I don't know which I was more heartbroken about—losing my marriage or losing my $4,000 Versace shoes? Anyway! So I sat on my best friend Greg's couch, opened my wet atlas to a random page, closed my eyes, and pointed my finger at an indiscriminate spot on the page. When I opened my eyes, I got up and went to the travel agent down the road to book a one-way ticket to Istanbul, Turkey. I arrived there four days later. I met a group of men my age who were vacationing there from Germany. Let me tell you! Those Germans, they know how to party. Turkish girls are very friendly, if you know what I mean!" Ashley bounced his eyebrows lasciviously at this point in the story and a rare smile cracked through his lips, showing stained teeth. He continued: "Gunter, Fonso, Bernard and myself went clubbing every night, befriending a few nice ladies along the way. We were having so much fun. One night, Bernard and I got completely drunk.

Bernard invited me to go midnight skydiving with him. Apparently, skydiving in the middle of the night is way more cool than during the day. I told him that I would love to try a new adventure, and anyway, there weren't any nice girls attracting my attention at the bar that night. The short end of the story is that my parachute didn't open when I jumped out of the flying airplane. However, the sensation of free-falling in the air for few minutes was absolutely exhilarating. When I hit the ground, I blanked out—I can't remember a thing after that. When I woke up from the coma in the hospital, the nice Turkish nurses told me that I had been there for two months already. They had to reconstruct my jaw and placed steel plates in my skull and legs. You have no idea how lousy healthcare is in third-world countries. I couldn't talk, walk or even go pee by myself. I had to stay for two more months in that filthy hospital until I learned to walk again. I lost tons of weight at that point. All the well-toned muscles I'd cultivated in the gym were bye, bye—even my six-pack. I used to look like a body builder and when I looked at myself in the mirror, I saw a scrawny skinny man with a deformed jaw. I still can't recognize myself in the mirror whenever I look at myself. The first thing I did when I could move my feet and fingers half-decently was to walk out of the hospital—still wearing a hospital gown and in bare feet—to the nearest Internet café. To my horror, I discovered that my Yahoo account had been disabled due to long-term inactivity. That account had held all my life! All the contact information of all the nice ladies I had met over 15 years. All of my business contacts. All of my electronic documents. All of my virtual identities. All of my avatars. Even my half-finished novel. My whole virtual universe had collapsed! All of it was gone. I groaned in horror in the Internet café like a wraith becoming aware of his lost humanity after 1,000 years of meaningless living. Everybody stared at me like I was a zebra dressed in a clown's suit at the zoo. Ten minutes of hurricane sobbing ensued before somebody called an ambulance. The paramedics took me back to the hospital. I would say that that day in the Internet café was the lowest point in my life. I had lost everything—my marriage, my physique, my Versace shoes (although I bought cheap knockoffs in Turkey for $20 to console myself). What devastated me the most was the loss of my digital life. There was nothing else for me to live for! I became nobody. And so I decided to come back to the U.S. and get a job at Snugoo, writing programs."

I am not sure whether the story is real or not, but Ashley does have a skewed jaw which makes him look like he had been in an accident, and he does walk with a limp. He is tall and gangly, and sports a pencil-thin mustache. Most of the time, I feel exasperated after hearing one of Ashley's stories. A sharp pain attacks the bottom of my right heel. I feel an urge to take off my shoe and massage relief into the afflicted area. Etiquette prevents me from putting into action that which, in my fantasy world, is most heartening. Ashley's stories leave me confused and apprehensive. I am certain that there is a way to make Ashley look at the bright side of life; however, saying positive things to him only triggers a flood of determination to prove his negative point of view. My initial efforts backfiring, I will resort to pursuing a different strategy: instead of pointing out the positive things in life, I reason that a subtle approach will be more useful. I will drop indirect hints. Eventually, Ashley will be influenced subconsciously.

Ralf

Right next to Ashley's desk is my co-worker Ralf's desk. The two are engaged in a perpetual conversation about nonsense. Ralf has an optimistic view of himself which I find disturbing, because it is misguided optimism. The first time I met Ralf in the hallway, I introduced myself and shook his hand. After polite greetings, Ralf challenged me to guess his age. "Most people are shocked when I tell them my age—go ahead! Look at me and guess my age." I examined his overweight figure, the protruding stomach and the grey hair around his temples, and the number "50" popped in my head. Then I thought it would be wise to be kind and flatter my new co-worker, and so guessed "40" instead. Ralf's eyes widened with shock at my response: "Most people guess 30, and are later surprised when I tell them that I am actually 46—that is very strange that you guessed 40, because I look much younger than my age." Ralf was vain about other things, as well, such as his intellect, attractiveness to women and abilities at work. Although I consider myself an optimistic person, I found Ralf's overestimation of himself irksome—especially when he brags about how irresistible he is to women, mainly because I find it hard to imagine that anybody could possibly be attracted to a hairy, overstuffed teddy bear. And it wasn't just his physical appearance that was a detriment to alluring the other gender; his personality missed charm the way the Sahara desert missed rain. Ralf likes to tell stories about how women are chasing after him and how he is always breaking women's hearts.

Yawn! I will believe it when I witness it!

Today's story from Ralf went like this:

There was Hilda. When I broke up with her, she camped outside my apartment building. She asked all the neighbors walking in and out of the building if they had any news from me. She would follow me to work. At Passover dinners, she showed up at my parents' house. She even wrote emails to my boss, begging him to intercede on her behalf. I felt so guilty breaking her heart that I decided to move to Israel for one whole year just to help her get over me. I am a complete atheist, and living in a Jewish state whose inhabitants speak a foreign language was pure suffering. I was missing Washington, especially those fantastic Cobb salads we get here. Do you know that you can't get a decent Cobb salad in Jerusalem? Mainly because bacon is forbidden in the Jewish tradition, and hence most restaurants won't serve it. So I endured for 12 long months away from all my favorite foods, eating falafel sandwiches instead—which I call "cancer balls." Over there, they fry in the same oil for months— and who knows if it's oil or diesel that they put in the frying pan, anyway? Where was I? Oh, yeah! I suffered for what felt like a decade, just to help Hilda get over me. So these days, I am careful and try not to be so charismatic. I don't like seeing the poor ladies agonizing. I don't want to move out of my favorite city again. I wish I were less attractive; I would have fewer problems. I sympathize with Brad Pitt—must be hard when you're both handsome *and* famous at the same time! Lucky for me, I only have the one whammy to deal with."

At least Ralf's self-delusion was not affecting my heel—a small blessing for which I am grateful. I only felt mild irritation in my left hip, which is easy to ignore. Although I admire optimism and positive thinking, bewilderment struck me whenever I came in contact with Ralf's opinion of himself. He was neither good looking nor in possession of one ounce of charisma. I had lots of experience in cheering up negative people. The novelty of bringing somebody down to earth to come to grips with reality intrigued me.

Childbearing Hips

I have gone this far into this story without describing my physical appearance. You probably think that this is a deadly flaw in the construction of my narrative arc. I assure you that this omission is intentional. I have discovered that what people don't know, they simply make up. I was hoping that your imagination would fill in the blanks in the parts that I left out. Perhaps you envisioned a young woman with chiseled facial features and an exquisite physique. Plump lips, athletic build, silky skin and cheeks that blush like petals of roses are all within the realm of possibility in a fantasy land where reality resides in far and exotic places.

Had this story featured Ophelia, Desdemona or Juliette, no such coyness would have been necessary. You would have been impressed with their beauty upon first sight. Each one of my friends is far better equipped to be the heroine of an epic tale on the likes of which future generations would write academic papers in order to attain Ph.Ds. in literature.

All tales featuring a heroine are written about beautiful women—this fact stands true in both Quari-ay-eh-ay and in the U.S. From Tolstoy to Flaubert, none of the brilliant authors from around the world had been able to expand their creative imaginations into a place where ugly women have interesting thoughts, nuanced feelings or committing acts of heroism—at least none that are worth writing about. I was worried that had I disclosed the inconvenient attributes of my genetically inherited material, you would lose interest in this story. So I delayed and delayed for as long as I could, hoping that I could hook you into the story enough so that by the time we had to confront this tricky issue, you would be sufficiently invested so as to be curious as to how it ends. Did I succeed? Will you stop listening to this story once you find out the next part?

Okay ... I am not exactly ugly; I would describe myself as being average looking. I am 28 years old, Caucasian, am 164 cm tall, and I weigh 75 kg. I don't consider myself to be fat, nor am I slim. I am big-boned and have been blessed with childbearing hips. I am certain that I am meant to be a mother at a certain point in my life, for why else would the universe endow me with such features? It follows that one day, I will attract a man into my life who will find me sufficiently attractive so as to want to father these children. I am perfectly happy with this destiny. Excessive beauty is somewhat of a hassle for other women.

My hair is chestnut brown. I like to keep my hair shoulder-length, but only because my hair is fine and looks bad when grown any further. A natural wave waltzes in my hair, softening angular facial features. It's a small blessing for which I am grateful. "Beautiful" is the description I would use for my eyes only ... yes, I am serious—I have long eyelashes, and my eyes contain a certain spark which delights me. "Ugly" is the description I would use for my legs; I have chubby calf muscles. Nobody would ever accuse me of having sexy legs without being seized by a king-sized laughing fit suitable for a Monty Python marathon viewing. People assume I am always wearing pants or long skirts out of an outrageous notion of modesty, but I am simply trying to hide my unsightly legs. I don't begrudge other women the luxury of wearing short skirts; I just have enough sensibility to know that immodest attire is not for me.

I supposed I could have made up a far more appealing persona—one that is more conducive to hooking you into this story. In addition to the fact that such a deception would be morally reprehensible to me, there is always the chance that we might meet in person and you would recognize me from this story and be inclined to doubt the truthfulness of the whole lot of it. For how would you know that I fabricated only the part about my physical appearance, yet committed to the truth in all other aspects? No, no—only the full truth will do.

So there you have it—the plain truth. Sometimes truth is neither beautiful nor ugly; it doesn't set you free; nor does it illuminate dark corners of the human condition. Sometimes the truth ... just is what it is. Plain, boring and hardly worth mentioning, yet lurking in the background like an ill-fitting stage set that you need to ignore in order to appreciate the performance.

This is not a love story. This is not a story where a pretty woman faces a dilemma and all her problems get solved upon meeting the right man. This is not a tragic story where a woman follows her passions and ends up dead or committing suicide, either. This story will be radically different from all the other stories about women that I know of.

I have set out to tell you a good story—a story that will uplift your spirit and hopefully inspire you. I have no idea what will happen next, and no guarantee that I will be successful in my quest. I only have this intuition to go by that this will be the mother of all stories. Let us look at the evidence at hand. Ever since I made up my mind to start upon my quest, my nightmare about the white snake has disappeared. That tells me that I am on the right track. Think about the unlikely ease with which I secured my job at Snugoo, given my lack of qualifications. It is a clear omen of great events about to unfold. It is as if everything in my life until this point has been nothing but preparation for this task: my job at Bookmark Books, my close relationship with Uncle Miguel, and my luck to be born in Quari-ay-eh-ay. I can feel destiny marching towards me like a herd of elephants, and nothing gives me more pleasure than the thought of sharing my findings with you.

You are privy to a unique peek into events that might make history. Who knows? Perhaps this might affect all of humanity. The sky is the limit! So hold on and don't give up on this story … I guarantee that you will be rewarded for your patience in the end. I promise to tell you all and unveil all secrets and discoveries that I make along the way. I will not hold back—not one gram.

I hope that I have convinced you that this is one ride you can't afford to miss.

Feather Dress

Thank you for sticking with the story. As a reward for your perseverance and since you might be feeling cheated by the lack of romance in my narrative, I will tell you the only love story that I like about a beautiful woman who solves all her problems by marrying the right man. There is a twist, however; she marries the wrong guy who turns out to be the right guy. It's hard to explain, but you will see. It's one of the many stories told in the book, *One Thousand and One Nights* or *Arabian Nights*. However, I didn't read this in a book; I overheard Uncle Miguel telling this story many years ago. It was a rainy August afternoon in Quari-ay-eh-ay. I was about 11 when my mother held me by the hand and together we walked towards Uncle Miguel's house. I was left in the TV room to be entertained while Uncle Miguel and my mother sat in the formal sitting room, chatting. Unbeknownst to them, I snuck up to the sitting room and eavesdropped on most of their conversation. I overheard my mother sobbing and saying something in mumbling sentences which I wasn't able to discern. Then I heard the measured and comforting voice of Uncle Miguel coming through. O what a gift? To be told such a story by the best of storytellers. I am certain that my mother felt honored on that afternoon. I felt privileged to capture this gem, even though I wasn't the intended recipient of it. It's possible that the story has been distorted through the act of the passing down of narrative tidbits. Conformity to the text doesn't concern me. It's a good story, and I will attempt to tell it to you in the same fashion in which I heard it. As I matured, I grew to appreciate the story further. Today I see a deeper meaning in it.

So here it is—the Story of the Lady With the Feather Dress:

Praise be to God, the forgiving and the compassionate.

Praise be to God, who knows all hidden things.

Praise be to God, who created the whole universe and managed to wedge his mercy into every tiny dust spec.

Nothing is so strange that it cannot be true. No story is so unlikely that it cannot be told. No lie has a place in a story, for every tale is a magnetic levitation train that leads to the capital city of the truth.

There are three types of people in this world. The first learn from experience; these are wise. The second learn from others; these people are happy. The third learn from no place at all; these, my dear friend, are fools.

This is the mother of all stories. The wise will understand it. The happy will delight in it. And the fools will be bamboozled by it.

A long, long time ago, in a faraway land, lived a handsome young man called Hassan of Basra. Basra, back then—the same as now—is a city in southern Iraq, located at the crossroads between the Mediterranean and trade roads heading towards China. Hassan was so charming that women from far and near competed with each other to capture his attention. He received gifts, love poems, party invitations and even (from the most confident of admirers) marriage proposals. Everywhere he went, he was lavished with sly winks, loaded smiles and attentions that made all other men present feel uncomfortable. What young man would not grow arrogant in light of such adoration? I beg you to contemplate that question. To the great dismay of all his lady fans, Hassan remained unimpressed. He courteously acknowledged each broken heart, with the dreaded "Let's be friends."

Hassan's mind was occupied with a different matter altogether—he was bankrupt. Zilch is what he found in his money sack after a lively escapade in the tavern one early morning. Penniless, broke—there were no more dinars. After squandering his entire fortune that had been left to him by his father on wine and gallant company, he decided to sail away to strange lands to seek new fortunes.

Some people have all the luck in in the world, no matter how foolishly they behave. Hassan of Basra was a member of the clan of these lucky clowns whom all of us hate yet secretly wish we could join. Everywhere he sailed, he met new friends and new admirers. Kings lavished gifts upon him in return for a charming conversation. Treasure, he effortlessly found one evening while wandering in an abandoned field. He kicked a rock for sport and found a trove of jewels. Just like that!

But there was something else that Hassan found on his adventure. Something that he didn't know he was looking for, yet as soon as his sight beheld it, he couldn't live without it. Gazing at the sea from a high terrace one night, he was struck by the graceful movements of a large bird who had landed on the beach. Suddenly the bird shed what turned out to be a dress made of feathers, and out stepped a beautiful, naked woman, who ran to swim in the waves. She outdid in beauty all human beings. She had a mouth as magical as Solomon's seal and hair blacker than the night. She had lips the color of coral and teeth as luminescent as strung pearls. Her middle was full of folds. She had thighs great and plump, like marble columns. But what captivated Hassan from Basra the most was what lay between her thighs: "a rounded dome, like a bowl of silver or crystal."

Smitten with love, Hassan stole the beauty's feather dress while she was swimming, and buried it in a secret tomb. Deprived of her wings, the woman became his captive. Hassan installed her in a palace back in Basra, showering her with silks and precious stones. But he couldn't entice not even a single grateful glance from the beauty. He doubled his charm and adorned his visage with his most radiant smile, but none of his usual magic held potency in this rarest of situations. Hassan went mad; he was at his wits' end—this was a new challenge, the likes of which he had never encountered before. Desperate times required desperate measures. Hassan wrote love poetry and learned to play the flute. He stood under the window of the object of his desire and serenaded her with tender words of affection that would melt even the nonexistent heart of a rock. But she just sighed, rolled her eyes and complained that his singing gave her a headache. Upon consulting with one of his wiser lady friends, he was advised to hold a party at his palace and introduce the lady with the feather dress to his adoring fans. This seemed counterintuitive to Hassan, but at that point he was willing to try anything. A lavish party was thrown, and nearly all the women of Basra and neighboring villages attended to behold the sight of the miraculous beauty who had enchanted their idol. They stood around in their finest clothes like a bevy of widows giving each other support in their darkest hour. During the banquet, the lady with the feather dress looked across the room. She saw women of different shapes, sizes, ages, social statuses and fashion sense. And they all had a single thing in common: they all wished they could be in her shoes. When she saw the look of envy in their eyes, something mysterious began to stir in her chest. Was it vanity? Was it the need to be adored? Or was it some other calamity to which we have not yet attributed a name? Who knows! Soon after the party, a wedding date was set. The honeymoon lasted for 40 days and 40 nights. Hassan became the happiest man on the planet Earth. She bore him two sons. After two years of blissful marriage, he relaxed his attentive tenderness, believing that she would never again think about flying. He started traveling on long trips to increase his fortune again, and was astonished to discover one day, when he returned from an adventure, that his wife, who had never stopped looking for her feather dress, had finally found it and had flown away.

At first she only wanted to try it on, for old times' sake. When she felt the wind in her face and sensed the flight motion in her body, a flood of yearning overcame her. Old memories began to rush through her mind. "I thought I was happy, " she said out loud. "I thought I had everything I needed."

Taking her sons to her bosom, she wrapped herself in the feather dress and became a bird, by the ordinance of God to whom alone belongs absolute might and absolute majesty. She walked with a swaying and graceful gait and danced and flapped her wings, flying away to reach her native island of Waq Waq. Yet before leaving, she left a message for Hassan: he could join her if he had the courage to do so. No one knew then, and still fewer know now, where the mysterious "Waq Waq"—land of faraway strangeness—is located. Arab historians such as Mas'udi, the ninth-century author of *Golden Meadows*, situated it in East Africa beyond Zanzibar, while Marco Polo describes Waq Waq as the land of the Amazons, or the "female island". Others identify Waq Waq as being in Madagascar or Malacca, and still others situate it in China or Indonesia.

Night after night, Hassan of Basra wept 'til he fainted. During the days, he wandered the streets like a dervish in a daze.

Two months passed and the perpetual bewilderment of Hassan continued until one day, an ancient jinni heard of Hassan's story through an intermediary. The jinni's heart was gripped with a rare sentiment of compassion, and it appeared before Hassan in the middle of the night to reveal the secret of the true location of the land of Waq Waq. Didn't I tell you that some people are just lucky? Unfortunately, I can't reveal to you what was said that night, for most men who hear of its location are irresistibly drawn to go there, yet very few can survive the experience. Suffice it to say that Hassan had to cross seven valleys, climb seven mountains, sail across an ocean and pass a river. Along the way he was beaten, robbed and even sexually molested when he was captured by a giantess and placed in a cage. Somehow, through some crazy miracle, he survived all and finally emerged half-dead in the lush gardens of Waq Waq, which is ruled by women and guarded by beauties trained in the art of archery.

A different visitor would have been dazed by such a sight and immediately been exposed as an outsider. Hassan, however, had eyes only for his wife and two sons, and as such was able to wander about unnoticed for weeks. He even made friends with the natives. One such friend, to whom he confided, informed him that his wife was not a mere inhabitant of the wondrous land of Waq Waq, but rather a princess and a sister to the queen. Upon visiting the royal palace, the queen felt outraged by Hassan's ridiculous request to garner an audience with her sister. The queen of Waq Waq laughed and laughed and laughed. "What woman would leave the land of Waq Waq and choose to live among the unrefined company of her own free will?" asked the queen, not expecting a reply. "You!" She pointed an accusatory finger. "With your dinky little palace in the puny city of Basra, where humidity makes your hair turn kinky, where sandstorms blind your vision and the heat drives you mad—and all that strange and disgusting food you eat." Each word was annunciated with careful attention to give it weight. Each word felt like a stone flung with the intent to hurt. Hassan was hastily thrown in a jail cell. Shackles adorned his wrists and ankles the way jewelry adorns a bride on her wedding night.

When Hassan's wife heard of his predicament, she was seized with a new kind of madness. Was it love? Was it compassion? Or was she simply touched that somebody was willing to risk life and limb for her? Who knows? She whipped out her feather dress and carried both of her sons and her husband back to Basra in her bosom.

And that is how Hassan finally learned that when a woman sets her mind upon a course of action, it is useless to stand in her way.

Letter From Desdemona

Tonight, I come home to find, to my delight, a letter from Quari-ay-eh-ay in my mailbox. It is from Desdemona. I run up the two flights of stairs to my apartment. As soon as I walk through the doorway, I take my right shoe off by stepping on the right heel with my left toe, and then repeat the same with the left shoe. My fingers refuse to break physical contact with the smell of my dear motherland. I rip the letter open and start to read hastily while still in the hallway.

Dear Nelly,

Oh how I miss your sensible presence at our weekly fruity talk meetings. Things are just not the same without you. Ophelia is growing more critical. Last week, she told me that ordering the same banana chocolate cream pie week after week proves that I am stuck creatively and unable to evolve. Can you believe that? I told her that the chocolate shapes drizzled on top of the whipping cream is always different and therefore gives me a new jolt of delight. She responded that I should think outside the box and allow myself to explore new venues. I sensed that there is something bothering her, and so to cheer her up, I embroidered a beige lacy blouse which I got at Isaac's store. I used soft lilac flowers with green tea leaves along the sleeves. She thanked me for the gift in a superficial tone and then implied that it looks like the blouse I gave to my mother on her birthday, thereby accusing me of uniqueness depletion. I didn't see her wear it, not even once—not even to the neighborhood's monthly brunch. The blouse I gave to my mother on her birthday was embroidered with violet flowers, not lilac. Perhaps Ophelia is color blind and requiring an eye test. Or perhaps she has memory lapses ... I don't know. One thing I know for sure, socializing with her requires even more grace than it used to. Dear Nelly, please write her a letter and find out what is wrong. You always had the magical touch that imparted good mood to those in dire need of it. As if all this were not sufficiently outrageous, Ophelia has recently been making me teas that carry a heavy ginger taste. When I tried one of her blends, the tea was biting my tongue. Complete overdose of ginger! I think it was her way of telling me that I talk too much. Maybe she was trying to paralyze my tongue with her concoction. I pray that you judge for yourself who is creatively stuck. Naturally, I told her that I loved her tea and that it gave my tongue an energizing buzz. I should buy her some pants that are made of itchy and stiff material that would impede the circulation in her body, but I am not going to do that, because I am a nice person.

On a more positive note, Juliette is now experimenting with distilling camel's milk. Did you know that you can't import camel's milk from Saudi Arabia, because camels are becoming extinct there? However, she was able to find a source in Australia to sell her some. Juliette says that she will make a perfume that has medicinal properties. Sounds interesting, if a bit ambitious. I can't wait for the sniffing party that is bound to happen in a couple of months. I have already embroidered black pants with perfume bottles and camel shapes to give to Juliet when she unveils her new perfume. My new adventure is to embroider lace patterns on jackets. The backs of the jackets look like they are lined with lace, although they are not. It really is a unique invention. I am not going to give any of those jackets to Ophelia until her social graces return to her. I started working on the one that is for you, and will mail it to you as soon as it is finished. Since you are a bigger size, it might take a bit of extra time.

How is life in America? Tell me all about it. I hope you are able to get plenty of sleep.

With Love and Gratitude,

Desdemona Horlicks

Dear Desdemona,

Thank you for your letter. You have no idea how much I look forward to letters from Quari-ay-eh-ay. I miss home terribly, and hearing your news helps to appease the homesickness. Can't wait to receive your new invention of a jacket. I am sure that it will be a wonder of creation. I am glad that you did not buy itchy pants to impede Ophelia's blood circulation. There is nothing wrong with ordering chocolate banana cream pie week after week if the chocolate shapes on top give you a fresh sensation each time. I will write a letter to Ophelia to inquire about the ginger tongue bite incident; however, have you considered that perhaps her intention was to provide you with a preventative medicine for the flu which you suffer from in the winter months? It is completely possible that the overdose of ginger in the tea was done with a positive intention. You are right to feel offended at her not wearing your lilac embroidered blouse. Although I haven't seen the blouse, I believe that it is beautiful, as all of your creations are works of wonder. Your good taste is impeccable, and all of us wish we could have your clothing decoration skills. Perhaps Ophelia is saving the blouse for a special occasion. Don't worry—I will make inquiries and get to the bottom of the situation.

Thank you for asking about me. I am sleeping like a baby these days.

With loving intentions,

Nelly Nasah

●–o ●–o ●–o

Dear Ophelia,

I write to you late at night from my new abode in Washington, D.C., hoping that this letter reaches you in good health and spirit. Please accept my perfumed greetings that extend across the ocean my heartfelt longing for our friendship. Oh, how I miss being in refined company such as yourself. In this country, people not only don't take the time to decorate food, they don't even take time to sit down and enjoy it. It is not uncommon to see people rushing towards their work in the morning whilst consuming a hot beverage in one hand and a food item in the other. These mobile food articles are served in disposable cups and wrappers to facilitate traveling consumption. I will not attempt to describe the manner in which people dress, for it might disturb the balance of your beautiful constitution. Despite daily assaults on all of my senses, I have had the privilege of a few pleasant encounters. I have made the acquaintance of a new friend whom I call Elvi. He is usually tastefully attired and communicates in subtle gestures that make me wonder if perhaps a distant ancestor of his did not originate from our dear beloved Quari-ay-eh-ay. He is such delicate soul that conversing with him does not tax language facilities. Like all evolved beings, their mere presence is sufficient to replenish one's energies.

I pray that you inform me of your tea blending experimentations. I hear from Desdemona that ginger is an ingredient of recent interest. I presume this new twist in your creative journey is of interest to you for its medicinal properties. I wish I were there to taste and sample your fantastic innovations and be the happy beneficiary of such delicate infusions. It has come to my attention that a certain beige lacy blouse has come into your possession. How lucky for you to be lavishing in the loving gifts decorated aesthetically by a caring friend. As you wear your new blouse to next month's neighborhood brunch, do hold me in your thoughts for a few seconds— for I am in a faraway land, deprived of the delights of the company of such fine friends and the many gifts it brings.

With blended love and warm affections,

Nelly Nasah

A few days later, a package arrives in my mail. I guessed that it was the jacket that Desdemona had promised. I sat at my tiny dining table and opened the package, only to find pieces of paper and an assortment of art supplies. A letter from Mr. Trevrel was included.

Dear Nelly;

Bookmark Bookstore's customers are missing you. I have received many enquiries as to your whereabouts. People especially long for your unique bookmarks. I have taken the liberty of sending your favorite art supplies, in the hope that your spare hours might enjoy being filled with bookmark creation. I know the customers would be delighted to receive them. Do send me anything you make with haste. I hope your excursion to the foreign lands has brought you wisdom and maturity. Please know that on your return, your job at my bookstore will be waiting for you.

Sincerely,

John Trevrel

Unfinished Stories

Jack, the artistic director at Snugoo.com, was different than my previous boss in Quari-ay-eh-ay, Mr. Trevrel. Jack walks into the office at exactly 9:00 a.m., saying absolutely nothing on his way in, not even good morning to any of the staff sitting behind desks laid out across the office's floor plan. Stingy with words and dispensing them only when necessary, Jack had no tolerance for stories. All the staff at Snugoo.com learned over time to speak in concise sentences to Jack, and only when necessary, except for Ashley and Ralf. Whenever Ashley or Ralf began to tell one of their stories, Jack would raise his right hand to indicate "stop!" and would then say, "Let us please return to discussing work." No matter how many times Jack had stopped Ashley and Ralf from digressing into one of their personal trials, their compulsive need to at least begin a story would override their better judgment, leaving all sorts of stories hanging in the air without an ending. There was the "time I fathered a child with my best friend's wife..." that Ralf began to tell. There was the "I have never met my father and just two days ago, I received a phone call from a man with a hoarse voice claiming..." that Ashley began to tell in a meeting. Jack would interrupt and turn the meeting back to business, leaving the story dangling with unfulfilled potential. In these situations, I found myself tense. I was torn between my desire to hear the rest of the story and my sense of relief at not having to process yet another disturbing tidbit from the Ashley or Ralf puzzle. Sometimes I wondered why Jack had hired Ralf and Ashley, two people so opposite him in character. Even more worrying to me was the thought that perhaps I, myself, had something in common with the talkative pair, since I'd been hired by the same boss. Jack would sit in his office behind closed doors for hours. Ashley, Ralf and I knew that it was best to avoid knocking on his door. Once in a while, one of us would receive a phone call summoning us to Jack's office, wherein we would discuss work assignments. At the beginning of any meeting, Jack hands each of us a sheet of paper that states the agenda in numbered items.

Agenda for August 5th

In attendance: Jack, Ashley, Ralf and Nelly

1.   Report progress last week.

2.   Status update on bugs for Purple Gecko project.

3.   New work assignments for Tenco client.

4.   Introduce the new employee HR handbook.

In meetings, Jack spends most of the time staring at his laptop as he types meeting notes. He looks up from the screen once in a while to either stop Ashley or Ralf from digressing, or to respond to an unexpected reaction. All agendas and meeting minutes were maintained on the company server with records going back 9 years. I sometimes scan the old meeting minutes when I am bored; there are different employee names and different project names and clients. However, the theme is always same: bugs that need to be fixed urgently, new work assignments, new clients, and administrative tidbits. The scribe of all these notes is the one and only ... it's always Jack, with his numbered lists and concise sentences. From these old meeting notes, I am able to decipher that Ralf has been working for Snugoo.com for four years, and Ashley for a little over one year. My predecessor was called Terry. I am familiar with her work, since I had to modify a few of her website designs. Terry's work was mediocre, at best. Making slight modifications is painful for my constitution. Each time I suggest to Jack that I improve a website by redesigning it from scratch, Jack insists that there is no time for a major overhaul and commands me to perform the listed tasks with no added embellishments. Terry was fond of tables in her designs, which divided a web page into neat squares and rectangles in which to place information. She used the basic font Arial, which is abundantly seen all over the Internet, giving all of her pages a familiar, yet boring, look. She was also fond of light shades of blue and stylized icons that blended into the shading. The work of my predecessor is passable, but lacks any flair to distinguish it among the millions of other web pages on the Internet. At least she didn't commit any design faux pas by mixing mismatched fonts or colors. There were no jarring graphics or poorly designed layouts. Her designs were cogent, but not eloquent. It is easy to create harmonious designs when all style elements are kept at a base minimum of complexity. However, only a person with refined taste can create a complex cacophony of colors, fonts and graphics while still maintaining harmony and flow in the design.

In this meeting, I was assigned the major task of designing a new website for the Tenco client, providing graphic design and style elements. I walked away from the meeting with a skip to my step. "Finally! I will get a chance to show off what I am capable of," I thought to myself. Up until that point I had tweaked a few websites, changing a few graphics and altered the fonts. This was going to be the first time that I would get to show off my fine taste displayed in digital format without having to conform to the work of my predecessor. "I will show them what the daughter of Quari-ay-eh-ay can do", I murmured to myself, and readied to produce the best website design the artistic director of Snugoo.com had ever seen in his life.

"Tenco is a corporation that wants to embrace innovation in their next incarnation. Think corporate hip—nothing too obscure that the average American can't relate to; however, it must retain the feel and flow of being on the cutting edge. Unconventionally conventional," are Jack's instructions to me in an email. I read it with careful attention, savoring each word as I go. I repeat the phrases over and over, letting the requirements seep into my core fibers, hoping that what comes out will hold the essence while still showing my own particular flair. "Unconventionally conventional", I repeat the words in my head. "Same, but different. Familiar, but shocking. Old, but new." It's a difficult task, even for an exceptional American graphic designer; however, for a Quari such as myself, designing in paradoxes, creating harmony where nobody is able to foresee it, balancing the seemingly opposed ends of a spectrum, well, that will be a cakewalk for me.

That night, I went to bed fantasizing about how Jack, Ashley and Ralf would react when I finally revealed my design to them. Oh! Jack with his minimum attitude will try to restrain his amazement. Secretly, he will have to acknowledge the future web design revolutionary. Ralf will realize that he should refrain from his boasting and will be humbled in awe of his first glimpse of Quari-ay-eh-ay. He will learn to talk less and listen more. Ashley will behold the unconventional beauty and feel inspired into sensing a glimmer of joy in his heart. I then graduated to fantasizing of droves of Tenco employees who were unfamiliar to me yet, but I imagined generic American male and female faces in different states of amazement. "Who knows what other personal ailments will be healed in the next few weeks," I sighed with delight. "These poor Americans are complete virgins when it comes to aesthetic beauty and refined taste. They won't know what hit them. Their lack of exposure to anything remotely related to fine taste will work in my advantage and make my design that much more potent in its effect. People's hearts will burst open—who knows what might happen after that. I might end up replacing Jack as the artistic director of Snugoo.com. Over time, I might establish a fine taste ministry in this country to oversee that beauty and aesthetic balance roam the wild west of this land." That night, I dreamed that I was walking slowly in a lush green garden. The shrubs were neatly manicured and the grass freshly cut, emitting a pleasant green smell. Little purple lilies littered the garden wildly. There was a manmade river streaming down the middle of the garden in straight line, with little water fountains pouring into it from both sides. I skipped along, allowing a few trickles of water to drip on my head and cheeks. The water felt warm and refreshing. Out in the distance, I could see a peacock leisurely walking across the grass. Then I noticed a second peacock walking behind it. I approached them, then stood and observed them quietly while they sauntered around picking at seeds in the grass. The two peacocks seemed to be completely unaware of my existence. Suddenly the first peacock raised its head and looked straight into my eyes. The animal spread his tail in an impressive display. A blinding golden shine flickered in the sun.

I wake up the next morning in a joyful mood. "O, I love this dream," trying hard not to remember the dream that I had had in Quari-ay-eh-ay. "It is an inspiration!" it dawned on me. I had heard of people being inspired in their artistic endeavors, but it had never occurred to me that I would be one of those lucky inspired few. "This dream will be the inspiration for my website," I say loudly to myself while still lying in my bed. "The peacock and the beautiful blend of blue, green and gold colors of a peacock's feather will be the theme of my design." Now I am impatient to get to my office and begin pounding out my prized creation.

That morning, I get to the office before anybody else. When Ashley arrives, I initiate with a cheerful good morning. "Poor me, I am not having a good morning at all", Ashley responds with a moaning tone of voice. Then he proceeds to tell me :

My ex-wife and one of my ex-girlfriends met over coffee yesterday and discovered that for three years, I bought both of them the same Valentine's Day gifts. I got angry phone calls from both, calling me all sorts of adjectives that I don't want to repeat in polite company. The worst part is that Samantha left a post on Facebook calling me a European trash slut. So now Amanda, the nice lady I am trying to romance to catch into my net, is asking questions about it. I am not even European—I only stayed in Europe for one year. Trash is fine, but Euro trash slut, now that hurts.

I smile at Ashley, a broad, sunny smile, and say, feeling assured, "Don't worry, Ashley! Everything will work out for the best soon. You never know when you will encounter a miracle in your life." Then I wink at him in a knowing way

Ralf appears 20 minutes later and is breathing heavily, muttering curses under his breath. "That darned elevator is broken. I had to climb four flights of stairs!"

"You are this out of breath after climbing four flights of stairs only?" asks Ashley. "You need to come to gym with me and start exercising. Women totally go for men who are fit!"

Ralf is offended by the implication that he is out of shape. He shakes his head in disapproval. "I am optimally fit by nature; I don't need to go to the gym. I must be having a viral infection which is causing the breathing difficulty. Anyway! If I am any more attractive to the ladies, it might be dangerous to the mental wellbeing of our dear co-worker, Nelly."

I resent it whenever Ralf implies that I am attracted to him, especially when the complete opposite is true. Today, I am in a good mood and don't even mind Ralf's delusions. I smile back and cheerfully say, "I find it touching that you are attempting to spare me mental anguish—that is so sweet." Ralf is taken aback by my response. Normally I knock his physical attractiveness (or lack of it), which Ralf takes as further proof that I am attracted to him. "Women always try to pretend that they are not interested. The more they say they don't find you attractive, the more attracted they are," he would respond to my truth-telling attempts. Now that I am not denying it, Ralf is starting to get worried—it usually signified the start of passionate pursuit. "She doesn't look like the crazy stalker type," Ralf mumbles to Ashley, as if trying to assure himself.

Peacock

I situate my computer monitor to face towards the wall. I don't want Ashley or Ralf looking over my shoulder, taking sneak peeks at my design while I work on it. I want them to get the full dose, all at once, when it's unveiled. That way, the remedy will be most potent, I figure. I hunch over my keyboard and act engrossed in my work. Once in a while, I pause and cock my head from side to side and purse my lips forward while appearing to be deep in thought. The pauses only last for one minute or two, and then I resume clicking on my keyboard.

My heart desires to go all out for this design. I start by creating my own font from scratch. The eyes of the viewers of the website will be delighted at a most elemental reading level. I hand-draw all the characters of the alphabet in both upper and lower case. Imagining that each character is made out of bent peacock feathers, I shape each character on the screen of my imagination before I allow the flow to spill onto the page. With each character, I place the eye of the peacock's feather in a different location and facing a different direction. For a few of the characters, I had to use two peacock feathers; therefore, the letters S, E and F end up with two peacock feather eyes. Most letters have curvy lines with individual feather barbules jetting out at random places. After examining all the letters I've drawn, I realize that my favorite is the capital letter "I". I place the peacock's feather eye at the base of the letter facing upwards, and then I draw the feather barbule meandering from side to side as if the wind is blowing through them. The letter itself, I draw in a confident straight line with no curves to distinguish it from other letters. The combined effect of the erect letter with a dancing feather in front of it is pure majesty—sensual beyond belief.

At around 11:30, I sense a strange grumbling in my stomach and dash outside the office to go to the washroom, which is situated at the end of the hallway behind the elevator shaft. The doors to the elevator shaft are open, but instead of the usual beautiful comforting sight of Elvi, I see the top part of an elevator mechanism—there are wheels, cables and chains appearing from behind the opened door. Everything is covered in grease mixed with dust. I stop in my tracks, having forgotten about my need to go to the washroom. "Poor Elvi...he looks so sad," the thought jets into my mind. A sudden gloominess slithers around my heart. The euphoria that I had sensed just a few minutes ago evaporates like liquid nitrogen, in a quick audible pfft. Two mechanics in blue jumpsuits are squatting in the doorway to the elevator; both of them have black grease on their hands. One of them notices me staring at the elevator and says in a cheerful voice, "Don't worry, doll—there are no broken parts this time—only a jammed chain." I nod my head to indicate that I had heard the mechanic. To me, it seems like Elvi is having surgery, his intestines splayed open for everybody to see. The mechanics are the surgeons performing the operation. "This will be fixed in two hours," the other mechanic chimes in.

Afterwards, I return to my desk with my zeal dimmed and attempt to shake the disturbing image of injured Elvi out of my mind, but it just keeps popping back. Numerous attempts at daydreaming of elegant peacocks walking in a garden with harmonizing green, blue and golden colors in various shades help me to enter back into my productive zone—back to my web design. I avoid walking outside of the office for fear that I will again be assaulted with the disturbing image.

During my lunch break, I comment on Ashley's lunch with a disapproving tone of voice, hoping to prod him into improving his diet. "You are eating cold beans straight out of a can?"

"Yes, exactly the way my mother used to make it," is his astonishing reply. I laugh dismissively; I am certain that it was a joke, but Ashley is quick to affirm that no jesting is involved in his assertion. I am regaled with yet another dreadful story.

"When I was a kid, my mom would open any can in the cupboard and pour the contents on a plate, and that was dinner. White beans in tomato sauce was my childhood favorite because it tasted okay even when it wasn't heated. The canned beef stew had bits of congealed fat, which is disgusting to eat when it is cold. Tuna tastes too bland on its own. But beans in tomato sauce taste mighty fine with a piece of toast. My mama was a smart woman—she didn't waste time with cooking or housework. She figured out ways to make us stop bothering her. She told my brother and me that each time we asked for something, an angel in heaven would get his wings broken and would drop to Earth. Helped us become independent from a young age. I was supporting myself from the age of 14, earning a living walking dogs in our neighborhood. When I left home at age 16, my mom kept calling, saying that she would like to see me, but I knew she just wanted to ask me to give her money. I do send her money once a month, but I keep telling her to stop calling me because I can't stand hearing her voice. Each time she calls me I deduct 100$ from her monthly allowance; that way, her harassing phone calls become less frequent. Isn't that a brilliant way to get your mother off your back? I hardly hear from her at all these days."

Ouch! Heel pain ... no relief in sight.

I was at my wits' end. All of my usual methods to cheer people up were failing with Ashley. The harder I tried, the more Ashley felt compelled to tell me dark stories that depressed me.

By the time Jack left work, Elvi was back in order. I am able to enjoy a pleasurable ride to the ground floor, which I always look forwards to.

The next day, I am delighted when I find the peacock feather Ophelia gave me before I left Quari-ay-eh-ay. I was worried that I had lost it, but I found it tucked behind a few vases on my bookshelf in my apartment. Once at the office, I place the feather in an empty drawer inside my desk so that I can occasionally peek at it for a burst of inspiration without giving anybody even the slightest hint of what I'm working on.

After I scan the hand drawings to create digital images that go into creating the font, I face a new challenge. What to name my new font? I suppose I should call it "peacock", but that would be too obvious. I think I might call the font "Quari-ay-eh-ay," but then I worry. This is my very first font. It might not be my best work; I might create something more glorious in the future. I want to honor my country only with the best of the best. After a lengthy contemplation, I realize that I should focus on the effect the font will have on other people. The word "majestic" pops into my head. Yes! Majestic is the right name for this font.

Once the font is ready, I can't help but use it for typing. The capital letter "I" is so captivating, I find myself typing it over and over again to delight myself with its beauty. I I I IIIIIII IIII III IIIII. Pride is streaming through my veins like water through a man-made channel. I still have the rest of the website to design—a brilliant font on its own won't do the trick.

There are so many elements to a website design that need attention. There are icons, header images, list bullet points, color schemes, buttons and style sheets. Somebody with a less refined taste would do the obvious and design all of these in a peacock style. That would be too cheesy for a Quari. Instead, I chose the subtle approach of hinting at the peacock through indirect reference, and allow the Majestic font provide the answer. I go back to my drawing notepad to draw a lush garden where a peacock would enjoy walking, with seeds, figs and insects that a peacock would feast on, and a trickling water fountain where a peacock would drink. I am surprised at how little time I am spending touching the computer—so much of my work is happening inside my imagination and later on my notepad. Time with the computer is only at the very last stage. This website design is even more fun than making bookmarks in Bookmark bookstore. I am still using my rocks in a mayonnaise jar drawing technique, only on larger scale. As I draw one version after another of the peacock's garden, I realize I am drawing the place I have seen in my dream. I scan the three best drawings and then use them for all graphical elements required for my website design. My design is unique; it has the intimacy of something that is handmade. Although the end result is digital, it still retains a personal touch that distinguishes it from other website designs. My life is perfect. I am the happiest I have ever been!

Collapse

"How can something that is achingly beautiful inspire haunting ugliness?" I ask after I unveil my design to Jack, Ralf and Ashley. After the meeting, I sit at my desk to contemplate the peacock feather that has inspired a great deal in the last three weeks. At this moment, all it is evoking are deep notes of sadness. I place the feather under a stack of papers in the drawer so that I won't have to look at it.

"If blue and green were meant to be seen together, then bruises would look pretty," Jack told me at the meeting. Ashley spent most of the meeting laughing. The problem was that he brought instant noodles in a cup, which he prepared by adding boiling water. So while he was laughing, he would splutter soup and noodles all around, him making a mess. I kept handing him paper napkins, which I had tucked in my pockets, to rescue him. However, my efforts were insufficient, as he kept on talking, laughing and consuming his substitute for food. If only Ophelia were here to give Ashley one of her disapproving looks. I should take a video of Ashley eating and send it to Ophelia so that she would stop giving people a hard time about violating tea drinking etiquette. "Only a chick would produce something so frilly," was one of Ashley's spit-enhanced gems of contribution. Ralf didn't say much during the meeting, but he kept on making incongruous facial expressions which said enough on their own. His bushy eyebrows moved upwards and sideways in gestures of alarm. He opened his mouth wide as if he were a baby sitting in a high chair expecting his mother to feed him some mashed banana. Each time I showed a new slide, his head made backwards cocking movement as if he were a chicken about to regurgitate its food. At the end of the meeting, he produced a lengthy, musical "wow." "Wooooow! That was different" were the only words he manufactured. The most hurtful and elaborate were Jack's comments. This was the first time since I had met Jack that I saw him display emotion. His face turned red, and to the surprise of everybody in the room, he stopped clicking at his laptop and faced me, looking straight into my eyes in a sustained gaze. For the first time, he addressed me directly instead of transcribing his meeting notes. "This is the ugliest website design I have ever seen in my life. Our clients are refined people of good taste, not a hurly burly bunch who want to be dazzled with a cheap burlesque act. The function of a website design is to accompany the content that will be displayed on it. You are attempting to overpower and grab everybody's attention by punching them in the face. By giving the viewer a black eye, you got his attention, alright; however, he won't be reading the content. This is like my wife. Always fishing for compliments. Always attempting to grab attention with her provocative dresses and short skirts. Then, when I ignore her, she feigns an illness of one type or another to seize notice. One day it's a headache; the next, she thinks she is having a heart attack; then she is having difficulty breathing. On and on, it...." Jack stopped in the middle of his rant, realizing that he'd veered into the dark corners of his personal life. He went back to facing his laptop and read aloud the meeting minutes he was typing:

"Design to be simplified:

1.   Fewer colors

2.   Standard graphics

3.   Use one of Terry's designs as an example

4.   Hand-drawn font—out!"

After lunch, Ashley and Ralf sat at their desks and had one of their inane discussions that I loathed to hear. Ashley started by saying,

"How does that song go? You know—the one that starts with 'la la la da da la da la da da.'"

"Oh, you mean the one that sounds like that other one?"

"You got the idea—I do want the words, but not for that one—you know, the other one."

"It was on that show, with those people who did stuff."

"Like singing and stuff."

"Oh yeah, that's right...I think it won an award."

"Are you sure you don't mean the one that was featured on the show hosted by...oh, what the bleep is that guy's name, again?"

"Oh, that guy! Yeah, his wife was in that movie about a group of people fighting a corporation."

"Yeah, yeah! That guy—the guy with that thing on his face."

"And the song had a version in Spanish they used to play on some car commercial or a soap ad."

"I've forgotten the name of that woman from Madrid who did the song."

"Wait a minute! No—never mind."

"Madrid? No, that's not right. I'm sure it was that other capital of a country."

"You know, the country where they had that battle in that world war."

"You mean the guy with the thing on the face? I think we saw him at a concert once, in some big city."

"Maybe it was one of those Canadians—you know, with that food they all eat over there."

"Oh, right—that food made from that farm animal that people in civilized places think is too cute to eat!"

"That song, it's pretty deep. Like that movie where everything is normal but turned fundamentally upside down and at the end, you're left with a message in the back of your brain that gets you thinking about that topic you heard about on the news."

"How does that song go again? It's on the tip of my tongue".

"'Take these broken wings and learn to fly again'?"

"Bingo!"

"Yes!"

"Yes!"

"High five!"

"You're the best!"

Normally I just ignore their discussions, but at this moment I am particularly agitated. I feel a sudden urge to stand up and shout at the top of my lungs, "What are you fools talking about!?!! Are you two idiots capable of a single intelligent conversation?" To stop myself from losing my temper, I go to the washroom in order to wash my face and calm down. I can understand why Jack rejected my design. He must feel threatened because of the superiority of my taste. If he gives me the tiniest of a chance, I will supersede him in no time. He might lose his job, and so it's in his best interests that I only produce mediocre designs. I don't understand, however, why Ralf and Ashley sided with him. Both of them are computer programmers, and so my work isn't threatening to them. I understand that they need to side with the boss in order to not get into trouble; however, why did they have to side with him so strongly? Perhaps their lack of good taste is more severe than I thought. Their impediment is so crippling, they are unable to recognize it.

I wasn't able to get any work done for the rest of the day, and at exactly 5:00 p.m., I decided to go home. On my way down, I could feel Elvi's sympathy towards me. He seemed to be going down slower than usual, and he was sliding from side to side as if he were trying to sway me into comfort. I am sure that a beautiful elevator with brass doors and beautiful carpet would appreciate the beautiful design I had made. Elvi is the only beautiful thing in this ugly office, full of ugly co-workers, in an ugly city that is filled with ugly people who eat ugly food and live in ugly clothes. Now I have to face a real dilemma. I can either follow Jack's instructions and create a design that nauseates me, or I can insist on my design and then lose my job. Creating an inferior design is something that goes against the core fiber of my body. I don't want to humiliate myself. What would Uncle Miguel say if he saw me creating a website that is below standards? How would I ever be able to show my face again in Quari-ay-eh-ay?

The next morning, it is Friday. I savor my ride with Elvi and brace myself for a challenging day at work. All day I sit at my computer pretending that I am working, but really I am considering my options. Should I resign? I write several prospective resignation emails.

Dear Jack: I resign. I refuse to continue working in an environment that kills my creativity.

Dear Jack: You sit behind a closed door all day and you hire barely functional people so as to cover up your own incompetency. You are a lousy boss and a sad human being. I can't work with you anymore.

Dear Jack: I am sorry about the difficulty and pain you are experiencing with your wife. You deserve love like all of us do. I sense that you are projecting those feelings onto me, which is preventing you from looking at my website design in an objective manner.

I left all my prospective resignation emails in a file on my computer, opting instead to take the weekend to think it over. For one thing, I wasn't able to come up with the perfect resignation email that summarized elegantly what needed to be said on such an occasion. Plus, I need to consider my options.

I spent the rest of the day looking at my computer clock, waiting for it to be 5:00 so that I could head home. The time seemed to stretch like the chewing gum in the mouth of an 8-year-old girl.

On my way out, I tell Elvi about the trouble I am in. I hold the brass railing, and I can sense the sympathy he is feeling for me. That is when I realize I can't leave Snugoo.com. I might be able to find another job in another office—despite my lack of qualifications—but all the other offices have ugly, plain elevators that fit with everything else in this country. I would miss my daily encounters with Elvi. I simply have to find a way to make this work!

On Saturday, I go for a long walk in the park that is about five blocks away from where I live to contemplate my predicament. That is when it occurred to me to write a letter to Uncle Miguel. He's traveled abroad extensively, and probably knows how to handle the lack of taste refinement in foreigners. I bet he's encountered this situation before and can offer valuable insight. I rush home from the park, sitting immediately at my desk. On a sheet of white paper, I draw an outline of a maze. That way, when Uncle Miguel finishes reading my letter, he can tantalize his intellect by drawing a line that navigates through the maze. Then I proceed to write:

Dear Uncle Miguel,

My life, 'til this point, has been a complete failure. Ophelia and Desdemona are warring again. I tried my best to be my usual peacemaker and wrote both of them letters. I am afraid I only made things worse, and now they are not even talking to each other. Mr.Trevrel keeps sending me supplies to make bookmarks, which I don't have time to do. I don't know how to tell him this without hurting his feelings. Worst of all, my mission in America has been a complete failure. Both my boss and my co-workers at my new job suffer from severe taste impediment. I am being asked to create a nauseatingly plain website design that goes against my aesthetic moral fiber. Oh, dear Uncle Miguel, please help me. With your extensive travel experience and your unmatched style, how do I lift these degenerates I am dealing with out of their stylistic squalor and enlighten them towards a higher plane of exquisiteness?

With love,

Nelly

As soon as my letter was finished, I ran outside to mail it. I am certain that Uncle Miguel is going to impart some valuable advice that will make Jake change his mind. Right away, my spirit lifted; I knew that a solution to my dilemma was on its way. All I need to do for now is compromise just a little, do exactly what my imbecile boss is asking me to do—just for a little while—and then BAM! I will come at him with whatever secret weapon Uncle Miguel is going to provide me with.

Squalor

On Monday morning, I rush to work early. I want to be sure to have a private ride on Elvi to tell him my news. As soon as Elvi's brass doors open, a nauseating smell wafts out of the elevator. I get on anyway, but by the time Elvi arrives at the 4th floor, I can't wait to get out. Elvi must be sad in protest to the way I am being treated at Snugoo.com, and so he has decided to make a statement that would be noticed by everybody in the building. I do appreciate Elvi's sympathy, but he also deprived me of my lone pleasurable experience in this city. I wish he had found a different way to register his stand of solidarity with me.

When Ashley arrives at the office, he tells me that most likely a homeless person had decided to sleep in the elevator and ended up urinating inside the elevator, as well. I don't correct him, because it is best if people don't know about my special relationship with Elvi. I wouldn't want Elvi to get into any trouble. Then Ashley proceedes to tell me a story:

"This reminds me of the time I woke up to find myself laying in the back of a truck covered in urine. I smelled as bad as that elevator. I had no idea how I ended up in the back of that truck, nor where it was heading.

When I opened my eyes, I realized we were driving on some highway. When the truck stopped at a gas station, I snuck out of the truck and into the washroom, trying to clean myself up as best as I could. Luckily, my wallet with all my credit cards was still in my pocket, but all the cash was gone. The gas attendant informed me that we were on a highway leading to Chicago. It was 6:00 in the morning. I was expected at work at 9:00 back in Washington. Imagine the looks on people's faces when I boarded an airplane from Chicago airport headed towards Washington, .D.,C smelling like that elevator. That was one airplane ride to remember. I smiled like the Joker from the 'Batman' movie the whole way."

At work, I resurrected one of Terry's plain designs and began to tweak it. I changed the shade of blue to a more appealing azure color. I also decided to freshen up the icons, giving them a more 3D look by placing shadows around the outer edges. "Uninspiring" would be the best word to describe the quality of my activity at the office. Ralf arrived at work late and dragged Ashley to the kitchen, where they proceeded to whisper about two Argentinian women whom Ralf had met over the weekend. One of them is called Dora; I didn't catch the name of the other one. Hooting sounds were coming out of the kitchen, followed by quick hushes. "Sh sh sh! " I overheard Ralf instructing Ashley. "If Nelly hears this, she might feel jealous."

I envy Ralf for his delusional self-confidence. I wish I could walk around believing that all men were madly in love with me and that I am so irresistibly alluring, no man can escape my charms. I would be a much happier person if I weren't so painfully objective. Alas, my logical side doesn't allow room for self-delusion. In Quari-ay-eh-ay, we have a saying: "God have mercy on a man who comprehends his true worth," implying that when a person realizes how insignificant he is in the grand scheme of things, he is crushed by such a revelation. I, for example, realize fully that I am an entirely average-looking woman. At 28 years of age, I am considered a touch past my prime in Quari-ay-eh-ay. Towering a full head over Desdemona always gave me an eerie sense of pleasure. I have enough feminine charm to attract one good man into my life and start a family—and one good man is all I really need. My destiny hasn't cooperated yet, but that is okay—who has time for romance or family building when one is engaged in revolutionizing the Internet? I thank God that I can dedicate all my time and energy towards this worthy pursuit without the distraction of a nagging husband. I have the ample example of Desdemona to remind me why being single is its own peculiar blessing. Desdemona made the mistake of marrying a foreigner—against the wishes of her family and ignoring the advice of her friends, she went ahead and married Atwell from Iceland. Everybody told her that a foreigner might seem intriguing at first, but only a proper Quari man can bring happiness to the heart of a Quari woman. All of us tried hard to accept him out of love for Desdemona. I have to give it to Atwell—he does try hard to integrate into our society. He cross-stiches poppy flowers and heart shapes into delightful art pieces that he calls "Icelandic Poppy Blooms." They do look delightful. He also presses flowers into paper until they are completely dry, yet maintain their shape and color. He frames his pressed flowers and sells them. His flower creations are interesting despite their simplicity, and have become popular in Quari-ay-eh-ay. Although everybody has made an enormous effort to accept Atwell as part of Quari-ay-eh-ay, Atwell continues to feel self-conscious about his status as an outsider. Poor Desdemona is left the task of reassuring him constantly that he is well loved by the community. He cross-stitched a handkerchief with strawberries, heart shapes and doves, and gave it to Desdemona for their one-year anniversary with strict instructions that Desdemona must wear it next to her heart at all times to remember his love. What a burden this handkerchief has become over time. Whenever Desdemona has the misfortune to forget the darned thing, Atwell goes into a hysterical fit, accusing his wife that she doesn't love him because the embroidery on handkerchief is not good enough for a Quari. Desdemona then spends the whole night apologizing, crying and swearing that it is the most intricate of embroideries for a napkin she has ever seen. What an idiot Atwell is—allowing a tiny piece of cloth to terrorize his marriage. Once I was shopping with Desdemona for new shoes when she realized that she had left the cursed handkerchief in her bedroom. I had never seen such look of horror on anybody's face. She ran out of the shoe store like a lunatic in a frantic fit to retrieve the napkin before Atwell discovered it. Whenever I feel lonely and sad, I remember Desdemona's face in that shoe shop and I realize that being single is not such a bad option.

For the rest of the day, everybody is using the staircase to get in and out of the building, studiously avoiding Elvi. As much as I appreciated Elvi's gesture of sympathy, I had to follow the crowds, because I couldn't stand the foul smell. I hope that the building management will find a way to clean up the elevator.

On Tuesday morning, when the brass doors of Elvi open, an even worse smell attacks my poor nostrils. It seems that the building engineer attempted to disguise the urine smell by pouring a disinfectant all over the carpet of Elvi's floor. The smells of the disinfectant and urine danced an intimate Argentinian tango together and produced a bastard child that resembled neither. I thanked Elvi for his efforts to show support for the hardship I was facing, and then I apologized with tears in my eyes for not being able to take rides with him for the next little while until the bad smell was gone.

I felt agitated all day; not only was my brilliant design rejected by the imbecile boss, my single source of comfort taken away from me, but also I had to wait for Uncle Miguel's letter so that I would know what to do next. I had no choice but to try to spend the next few days occupying myself with pleasant activities. I found myself lingering in the park to and from work to replace my daily rides with Elvi.

Letter From Uncle Miguel

Dearest Nelly,

I have read your letter carefully and have spent two weeks pondering the answer. Please forgive the delay in my response, for I wanted to be certain to give you a considered answer to your request.

You are a brave young woman. Life has forced you to bear grown-up responsibilities at a young age. While other teenagers were chasing boyfriends, you had to deal with the grief of losing your dear mother, and later, the care for your ailing father. While your friends went to university and enjoyed one party after the other, you stayed home to change dirty sheets and comfort a desperate middle-aged man. In truth, I feel a sense of regret and shame for not helping out during those difficult years. I was busy tending to my palatial duties, obsessed with furthering my career. I neglected to aid my lone goddaughter and best friend in her hour of need. I watched you deal with such adverse situations with bravery and good humor; I greatly admire your spirit. When your father finally recovered from his diabetes and depression, you had to start your life without the benefit of a university education; yet, you managed to educate yourself in the finery of Quari etiquette on your own, using the weapon of self-determination in place of teachers and university professors. To you, my dear goddaughter, I tip my hat. You have achieved much and soldiered on where many others would have been crushed. There is no doubt in my mind that you can achieve anything you set your mind to.

I have read about your troubles with Juliet, Ophelia and Desdemona, and I will set up a meeting with the three of them to chastise them for being boorish, inconsiderate airheads. Instead of lending you a supporting hand while you toil away in a foreign country, they pile on their own troubles. I think all three of your friends need to grow up and figure out how to solve their own problems, instead of relying on you to keep the social dynamic flowing. It's about time somebody gives these three a piece of his mind. So please don't worry about it at all; I will deal with it—you focus on building your new life in America.

As for Mr.Trevrel, I feel angry to hear that he has been troubling you abroad with his crazy bookmark obsession. Why doesn't he stop selling books and focus on bookmarks, since it is the only thing he cares about? When was the last time you saw Mr. Trevrel reading a book? For a bookshop owner, the man lacks interest in books. Please do not worry yourself with him at all. Simply clear your mind of any thoughts of Mr. Trevrel. I will have a word with him. He will never bother you with his bookmarks again.

Now let us focus on the most important aspect of your letter—how to get your co-workers and more importantly your boss to accept your refined Quari taste. I know with a certainty that your design is far superior to any design they have ever witnessed in their lives. You are my goddaughter, and I know what you are capable of. Please remember that foreigners feel intimidated by the enormity of our good taste. Surely, you must sympathize with their predicament. Imagine a poor man who has been starving for months and months, or maybe even years—he is emaciated. If you attempt to feed him a plate of stuffed grape leaves, roasted lamb and cooked yogurt sauce, you might kill him. You first start by feeding him a light broth, then perhaps a few boiled vegetables, then perhaps some plain oatmeal. Over time you begin to introduce some real food, but gradually. The poor man's stomach needs time to adjust to food. It is the same thing with beauty. Those poor foreigners were not so lucky to behold beauty on a daily basis as were we. Being subjected to it all at once might cause their nervous system to collapse. They have every right to dread your finest creation; it is self-preservation in action. You need to start with making a light broth. This task you have taken upon yourself requires patience. You need to take one step at a time. Don't present them with the stuffed grape leaves when their senses have been starved since birth.

Love and Admiration,

Miguel Legena

"Patience! Patience!" I scream aloud when I read Uncle Miguel's letter. "Is that the secret weapon I have been waiting for?" I feel despondent and confused. "How much patience do I need?" I talk back to the letter as if Uncle Miguel can hear me through a secret portal. "One month? One year? A decade?" I am supposed to be famous already and on my way to chairing the good taste ministry;', instead, I can't even get a single design to see the light of day. I have always admired Uncle Miguel, but I am certain that patience is not the right way to achieve my goal. I am glad, though, that he will get Mr. Trevrel to stop pestering me about making him bookmarks in my spare time. At least one good thing came out of corresponding with Uncle Miguel.

Silence

I am dumfounded. Stuck. I have no idea where to go next. This story is not proceeding the way I had intended it to. I don't know what to say or how to explain; I am experiencing strange feelings. Even worse are the sensations in my body, such as lightheadedness ... oh, forget it! I am not going trouble you with what is going on in my life. This story is over. I apologize for wasting your time. Please go away and forget about me. I have nothing more to say.

I told you there is no story ... just Go Away!!

Reboot

I don't know what this is any more. I wanted to tell you a story that would inspire you. A story about a woman who transforms her life through her own determination and hard work. A story like that of Tania Tulip, only magnified tenfold. You can review the story of Ms. Tulip at the end of the second chapter. I wanted to tell a story similar to Tarzan and Jane—only in that story, I would be Tarzan. The role of Jane, I happily relinquish to anybody. You can play the role of Cheetah. Did you notice that Tarzan spent more time talking to Cheetah than to Jane? The truth is, I enjoy speaking with you for some strange reason. Although this telling has lost its purpose, I feel an urge to continue. My initial promise to you is revoked, except for the part of telling you only the truth. Perhaps the rest of this will be continuous boring rants about nothingness. I might go on and on about the endless jibber jabber of Ashley and Ralf. I find myself no different from the two of them—aimlessly spewing out words that scatter into the void of bewilderment along with the ache of loneliness. I might build one bland website design after the other. Or I might fill the time telling you about microscopic things that are no different than your everyday meanderings. The small moments of life stuff: I went for a walk; I ate a roast beef sandwich; I wore my favorite blouse to work ... etc. Surely your life is full of such exquisite gems. I promise nothing but the truth. I have no clue why you are still listening to me. But here you are, so I suppose I might as well fill the time with something. Isn't something always better than nothing? Using my newly acquired high-tech speak, this story is getting a reboot. Here comes story 2.0. I am beginning to comprehend why many stories are written about seductive women. In such stories, even when nothing happens, at least there is romance to talk about! Somebody told me that Washington, D.C., is full of important gentlemen who exact vast influence. Had I been fetching in appearance, there would be a handsome man whose eye I would have caught and I would have something of note to report to you. "Today I received a flower basket from X," I would be able to report to you, and elicit a meager bit of intrigue. Unfortunately, average-looking women need to actually have at least one accomplishment under their belts in order to be story-worthy. No such accolades are in my immediate forecast.

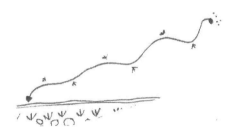

I feel that there is plastic lining under my skin, covering my whole body, and it is pressing me inwards while my skin is pulling outwards. A squeezing sensation fills me with compression the likes of which any pressure cooker would comprehend. The loosening of the skin is flighty with lightness. I am a heavy feather wanting to float in the air, yet tumbling down like a rock. Oh, what nonsense I come up with.

Please don't ask me about what happened in the three weeks I wasn't talking to you. That is my business. My silence is my cover. My chaos is my freedom. It is enough that I tell you that I had a difficult time, and leave the rest to your imagination. I will tell you one thing from these missing three weeks that is lighthearted. I found a book with an orange cover on a park bench that had been left behind or maybe forgotten. A creative non-fiction softcover titled, "Don't Shoot! ... I have another story to tell you." Isn't that a great title for a book? I wish I had thought of it myself. Only my book would be called, "Please Shoot Me! ... I have no story to tell." Ha ha ha ha ha ha. I enjoyed reading the book. The author has had an interesting life, and in the book, she recounts anecdotes from various parts of her adventures in a creative manner. Clearly she is much smarter than I, because she told her story after the fact, once she knew for certain that she had a concrete tale in hand. I wish I had been wiser and delayed my storytelling until all the angles had been calculated. My enthusiasm is now rebranded into foolishness. "To foolishly go where every woman has gone before" is my new motto.

Spinach Pie

It is raining. I walk briskly to the office this morning. To my delight, I discover that the carpet had been ripped from Elvi's floor, exposing untreated wood. Elvi looks a touch underdressed, but at least the smell is tolerable. There are a few traces of that weird tango that took place three weeks ago, but I will be able to tolerate it. My umbrella is dripping water, yet Elvi seems happy to see me despite his current state of undress. I greet him with a cheerful "good morning," and he sways side-to-side, clearly happy with our reunion. I tell him my bittersweet news, about Uncle Miguel's advice to make soup broth. "What do you think, Elvi? Should I follow my godfather's advice?" Elvi jumps and jerks, and I nearly jump with him. Then his door opens wide onto the fourth floor. "Are you telling me to just get going? Is that a 'yes'?" That is when his doors began to close tentatively but then opened again with a gentle nudge. "I understand, Elvi," I whisper to my beautiful friend. "Indeed, sometimes we need to do things which we find repulsive in order to get the things we really want. That is why victory will taste that much sweeter when it is attained in the end."

Sitting at my desk at the office, I am trying my best to make the mildest soup broth when I hear Ashley arrive in the office, murmuring words of complaint about the rain: "I curse this rain!" He spits out the words as if they were sunflower seed shells . Then he turns to me and explains, without any greeting: "Whenever it rains like this, my hip joints begin to ache. My theory is that the steel plates that have been placed in my right leg conduct electricity whenever there is enough moister in the air. It transfers the pain signals from my right toe, which is constant, into the tissue that surrounds my sternum, causing a pain transference effect." Ralf arrived at the office breathing heavily. Only this time, it wasn't because he'd taken the stairs, but rather because he'd ran all the way to work. "Eh, eh, I ran to avoid, eh, eh, getting wet, eh, eh, it's just pouring outside. Eh, eh," he forced the words out while wheezing.

Ashley jumps up in animated way and starts shaking his right index finger in Ralf's face: "That is why you got soaked wet—the faster you run in the rain, the wetter you get." Ralf is able to collect his breath and declares, in absolute terms: "That is scientifically false!" He pauses to swallow all the phlegm that no doubt is collecting in his mouth, and then he continues. "The faster I run, the shorter is the time I spend exposed to the open sky and the lesser is the exposure to the rain."

Ashley laughs. "That is what the uneducated masses think, but your theory assumes that the rain falls in a perfect vertical line, which most of the time it doesn't. Consider the wind direction today; I would say that the rain was falling at a 30-degree angle. That means that the faster you run, the more water you catch."

"Oh, what utter nonsense!" declares Ralf, exhibiting a type of passion I had never before seen him display. "What type of an engineer are you?" He mocks Ashley with a derogatory tone of voice. Ralf grabs a blue marker and heads towards the whiteboard that is situated right next to the front entrance of Snugoo. He draws diagrams and writes mathematical formulas to prove that running in the rain exposes him to lesser moisture.

Ashley marches behind him, standing there and listening to Ralf's argument with his hands crossed in front of him, but before Ralf is able to finish his argument, Ashley snatches the marker out of Ralf's hands and begins to draw his own diagrams and formulas, all the while spouting something about velocity, area of impact, speed of light and pi. The marker snatching goes back and forth with further animated discussion. Each one is trying to defend his engineer ego from getting bruised. Their voices get louder and louder until both of them are shouting at each other.

I don't understand half the scientific things they're talking about, but for some reason, I find myself interjecting in the middle. A lapse of good judgment on my side? "Fellows, fellows, I have the conclusive proof of what is the best method to walk in the rain while avoiding the greatest amount of moisture." Both Ralf and Ashley look surprised. This is the first time that I have participated in one of their useless discussions about nothing. I march over towards the whiteboard and gently take the blue marker out of Ashley's hand, which he surrenders willingly. I then take the dry eraser and wipe away all the scribbles that both of them have left on the whiteboard. There is a pregnant silence in the air; both of them are waiting with anticipation to see what I am about to say. In a slow and deliberate manner, I write on the board: "The best way to avoid getting wet in the rain is to carry an umbrella." I face both of them and say, "the proof of that theorem is this: I am the only one who walked to work with an umbrella today, and I am the only one who is dry right now." Both Ashley and Ralf laugh with mild amusement at my attempt to settle their discussion. Ashley grabs the blue marker from my hand and proceeds to draw a formula that estimates water flow based on the speed at which water drops from the sky. Ralf interjects to correct a coefficient.

I go back to the witch's brew disguised as benign nourishing liquid on my desk. A warm glow envelopes me after that, but it doesn't last long.

At lunchtime, Ralf approaches my desk and suggests that the whole office should go out to lunch together. I see this as a friendly gesture, indicating that Ralf is attempting to develop social skills. I reply with an enthusiastic "yes."

Lunchtime comes. I discover it's just Ralf and me heading out the door. "Where are the rest?" I nervously inquire.

"I asked everybody in the office, and you are the only one who said 'yes'," replies Ralf.

"Oh, no!" Alarm bells rise in my chest. I am afraid that this little outing might come off as some sort of a romantic endeavor. In desperation, I ask Ashley to join us, but he points at the Twinkies sitting on top of his desk. "I brought one of my favorite lunches from home," he says, beaming a big smile in my direction as if he were declaring his love for the factory-manufactured pastry. "The company that makes Twinkies filed for bankruptcy protection two days ago. When I heard the news, I had a full-blown anxiety attack. Can you imagine a world without Twinkies?" Ashley develops a tone of voice whenever he is about to tell a story from his life. It reminds me of the movie, "The Exorcist." In a horror movie, Ashley would be the voice of evil. I would be the character jumping out the window to save the world from hearing it. "Then I decided that I am going to buy Twinkies in bulk and eat them every day, just in case they stop making them in the future. That calmed me down."

I have no choice but to face lunch with Ralf alone. In a horror movie, Ralf would be the detective who attempts to find a rational explanation to the carnage, completely clueless that he is a puny sidekick in an irrational plot.

Ralf suggests that we go to a restaurant called "Teezo's," which is only a few blocks away from the office building. I am certain that anything Ralf chooses will be dreadful, but I go along without any objections, allowing Ralf to lead the way. "Modern Mediterranean Grill," Teezo's store sign announces to all passersby. Inside, an elderly gentleman with a big moustache and grey hair greets Ralf with a warm handshake, and seats both of us in the middle of the place. From the way he is ordering all the servers around, I guess that this is Mr. Teezo himself. It appears that Ralf is a regular here, since the staff all know him. The place has a cozy feeling. The walls are painted an earthy red. Olive tree branches and olives are stenciled all around. Pictures of the Mediterranean ocean are hanging on the wall alongside hand-painted clay plates. It is nowhere as close to the fine décor displayed in a Quari restaurant, but somehow I am surprised at how pleasant the place looks, considering the fact that Ralf chose it. I imagined that Ralf would be a regular at a little hole in the wall—the type of place where you might find grease stains in place of paintings.

The menu arrives. I find myself staring at words I don't understand: Calamari, Spanakopita, Dolmadakia, Saganaki, Tzatziki, etc. It all sounds intriguing, but I have no clue what to order. I am too embarrassed to ask what any of these dishes are, because I don't want Ralf to think that I am a small-town hick. So I say, nonchalantly, "You seem like a regular here; what do you recommend?"

"The Spanakopita is to die for," declares Ralf enthusiastically. "It is like no other Spanakopita you have ever tasted!"

Since I have never had Spana-thingymajig before, it is certainly going to be like no other I had had before it. I have rarely gone to restaurants since arriving in the U.S.; all my food experiences have been hugely disappointing. It is the American way to plop some food on a plate and present it as-is.

"Have you guys decided?" asks our waitress cheerfully.

"I will have the Spanakopita." I point to the menu item while ordering, just in case I am pronouncing it wrong. Ralf orders the Spanakopita with a side order of roasted lamb. He licks his lips while ordering, as if he can taste his food already. After our menus are taken away, I find myself looking awkwardly at my hands and trying to think of a way to converse with Ralf, but my mind is drawing a blank—I have no clue what to say.

To my great relief, Ralf starts the conversation by talking about his high school years: "I always wanted to be a computer programmer. When I heard that I could get free pornography on the Usenet, I got myself a Commodore 64c. I was cruising the alt.binaries every day. Those were the good old days—you would download a picture and sit there waiting for ten minutes for it to be rendered one line at a time. In a certain way, it made the experience more enjoyable."

Ralf continues to tell me about the virtual adventures of his youth, but I tune him out. It all seems as dull as watching paint dry. When our food arrives, I feel stunned. It looks delightfully presentable! There is a filo pastry pie on my plate, stuffed with something. On the side, there is a colorful fruit salad with strawberries, blueberries and an orange fruit that is cut out into the shape of a star—it is pleasing to the eye. The plain color of the filo pastry contrasts with the fruit salad. Then there is a thick yogurt that has shredded cucumbers and dill—everything looks green. Again the green matches fantastically the colors of the fruit and the plain filo pastry. The dish certainly would get an "A" for color combination. Everything is sprinkled with chopped parsley and carrots. Although there is no food decoration involved, I feel my eyes feasting for the first time since having left Quari-ay-eh-ay.

"What's the matter? Don't you like your food?" Ralf interrupts my enjoyment.

"No—everything is great; I am just taking the time to enjoy what my food looks like."

Ralf's plate looks exactly the same as mine, except his has a large, steaming hunk of lamb, which throws the visual out.

"Look!" I point at the fruit salad on his plate. "Somebody made the effort to cut out star shapes in a fruit—isn't that beautiful? I would like to ask the chef how he cuts the shape so perfectly." I was hoping to draw Ralf's attention to the important things.

"That isn't cut out," comments Ralf. "That is a star fruit—it comes in that shape and you just have to slice it."

It somehow seems less magical, now that I realize that the chef didn't labor for hours cutting out star-shaped fruit.

"Anyway!" Ralf interrupts my visual appreciation again. "Who cares what it looks like? Just taste it!" Ralf grabs his fork and tears through the roast lamb like a savage.

I pick up my fork and cut a portion from the filo pastry pie, electing to leave the fruit salad 'til the end. I place the first bite into my mouth, and am dazzled! The pastry is filled with cooked spinach and some type of white cheese mixed with lemon juice and mysterious herbs. It is a divine taste. The cheese is melting on my tongue right before the spinach taste is about to hit my taste buds, creating a unique fusion the likes of which I have never before experienced. The taste is delicate yet bold, balanced in ways that are hard to describe in words. The happy tingling sensation is warmly travelling from my tongue down millions of cells in my body, sending a pleasurable sensation which transports me into a dream land, where I am walking around a lush garden. I stumble into a maze built by shrubs. I am walking close to the edge, not caring about the fact that I am lost; my fingers are lightly touching the green leaves that are sticking out, causing a delightful tickling sensation in my fingers. That is when my pleasure fantasy is interrupted by Ralf's gruff voice: "Nelly! Nelly! Are you listening to what I am saying?"

I am startled at first; I want to go back into the shrub maze. It takes me a few seconds to regain my composure. I finally respond sheepishly, "Sorry, Ralf! I got lost in the good taste of this spinach pie."

Ralf seems pleased by the fact that I am enjoying my food. "Yes—didn't I tell you the food here is to die for?" Then, without missing a beat, Ralf dives back into the monologue about his youth. "Back in the day, I was a formidable hacker. My moniker was 'blue reaper'."

I know it is a mistake to pay attention to anything Ralf says, but I ask, compulsively, "What is a hacker?"

"Oh, you don't know what a hacker is? Where have you been living—the moon?" Ralf's mocking makes me regret my attempt to interrupt his favorite speech topic (himself). "A hacker is somebody who finds weaknesses in computer programs and exploits them to show off his computer programmer genius. By leaving a mark behind, a hacker makes sure that other hackers know what his exploits are, creating a competitive environment. I started by hacking into the university system and changing my own student record, and then I graduated to hacking into NASA's VAX computers. I changed all the pictures of all their astronauts to a picture of a grim reaper dressed in blue instead of black, which is how I got my hacker name at the time. Cyberspace was abuzz with my latest exploits. All the other hackers were attempting to imitate me. All this was long time ago, before the Internet..."

I interrupt him again. "Does this mean that a hacker can change a website without the consent of the admin?"

"Yeah!" retorts Ralf enthusiastically. "If you had permission, there would be no point."

"So how does one become a hacker?" I wonder out aloud.

"You have to have a special touch for playing with code. It's an art form as well as a science, but don't worry your head with such complexities, Nelly—this is not something for nice young women such as yourself."

If only Ralf knew how condescending he sounds each time he tries to give me a compliment. I try to focus on my amazing food and place more effort into tuning him out so that my enjoyment will not be spoiled with all the stupid things coming out of his mouth. I make sure to smile and nod politely every ten minutes or so, so that he won't interrupt my bubble of bliss by insisting that I actually listen to him.

The rest of our lunch goes well. I am rather surprised with how much I actually enjoy my lunch with Ralf. Perhaps he does have a small smidgen of good taste inside him, after all; otherwise, he wouldn't have selected Teezo's.

Just when I'd lost all hope, a flicker of it shines through to show me that I will be able to reform the likes of Ralf.

Insekab

Tonight I go to bed feeling inspired on two fronts. My taste buds are inspired by their new culinary adventure, and my mind is inspired by a new idea: A hacker is what I will become. How strange that Ralf, of all the people in the world, is responsible for both inspirations. I will place all of my energy into learning how to crack websites to install my own designs. How hard can it be? If Ralf was able to do it when he was a university student, surely I can figure it out. Sometimes when the level of ignorance is so high, one must liberate a nation of people against their own will. One day, people will thank me for taking this initiative. But for now, I must cover my tracks and be careful not to get caught—which reminds me that I need to come up with a moniker. Okay; I must think hard. This name that I will be known by must capture the totality of my fine taste energies that will be poured out into the world and shared freely like a gift. In the ancient Quari language, which is no longer used except by religious leaders on high holidays when they would give sermons that nobody understood but everybody would nod their heads as if they did, "Insekab" means "a pouring out," and it is the perfect name for somebody who is about to pour herself out on the Internet. Since my job just became boring, I will do Snugoo.com work for 2 or 3 hours a day, and spend the rest of my workday learning how to become a hacker. While I am working on my computer at my desk, nobody will figure out that I am not doing company work. Luckily, I have already positioned my computer's screen away from prying eyes, which means that nobody will be able to see what I am doing. Most people don't do more than three hours of work during the day, anyway—take Ralf and Ashley, for example; they spend hours every day discussing their imaginary romantic adventures and other useless subjects. Snugoo.com is lucky if it gets a solid two hours of work from each of them. To save time, I will recycle old Terry's designs one after the other with just a few tweaks here and there, and most of day I will expend working on my own escapades. This is so super exciting to me.

The next morning, I wake up bright and early and head to the office, hoping to have some alone time with Elvi so that I can tell him my plan. Elvi opens his doors wide as soon as he sees me. Inside his wide embrace, I divulge all my secrets. Elvi rocks gently. The soft ta-tuk, ta-tuk sound he makes as he moves is soothing. I know that Elvi is proud of me. My feisty insistence at not giving up brings us closer.

In the office, I divide my day into two chunks. Before lunch I do my own work, and after lunch I do company work. That way, I do the most important parts while I am at my most creative—the morning. I proceed to teach myself how to break into websites so that I can change the design.

That morning, Ashley comes up to my desk and starts telling me one of his stories. "Hey, Nelly, did I ever tell you the story about how I got my best friend's wife pregnant and then sacrificed my own happiness by refusing to marry her because I knew that would break my friend's heart?" Without stopping to receive any response from me, he continues on. "It all started when one day, Hailey arrived at my door in tears."

I was completely disinterested in what he had to say, especially since I was engrossed in reading about SQL injections, which is a special technique hackers use to fool websites into thinking that a legitimate user is logged in.

I notice Ashley's right hand. His middle finger and index finger are permanently stained brown. I interrupt him mid-speech. "Hey! Ashley, why are your fingers brown? You must be involved in some artistic pursuit that causes that. Perhaps you stain wood, or paint with oils?" I blink my eyes mischievously at him.

Ashley lowers his head, and in a low tone of voice, tells me that the stains are from smoking cigarettes.

"You mean you smoke so many cigarettes every day, the nicotine has permanently stained your fingers?" I couldn't hide my disgust at the notion.

"Way to point out the obvious, Nelly!" Ashley looks down to his feet and shuffles towards his desk, having forgotten the rest of the story he was about to tell me. Yay! Right heel pain averted for the day. I am glad I can get back to my SQL injections, but a little twinge of guilt pulsates in my abdomen. Who knew that you could hurt Ashley's feelings?

I spend the next two weeks learning everything I can about breaking electronic security walls. Since my objective is only to alter the design but not any content, my task is easier than I'd originally thought. If I can crack into the website administrator account. guessing password, that is all that is needed. Turns out that most people use similar passwords that are easy to guess; for example, "password," "123456," "qwerty," etc. When that fails, I leave a simple script running overnight, attempting a long list of passwords until one does the trick.

These days, you can learn anything for free on the Internet if you are willing to spend the time searching for the information. Learning hacker tricks is no harder than walking through a shrub maze—you have to try several paths, but sooner or later, with some patience, one of these paths leads to the desired destination. The best part is, even when encountering a dead-end, a walk among the hedges is still enjoyable.

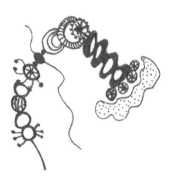

At the weekly team meeting, I show everybody my design. Jack looks surprised at my level of compliance. The design is everything he'd asked for—bland and boring. Nothing there to capture any attention or inspire the slightest feeling, except for boredom. He even utters a compliment, which is the first time I've heard him praise anybody or anything. "Well done, Nelly," he says at the end of my presentation in a matter-of-fact voice, as if he were saying, "The weather is rainy today" or "I think I need an extra cup of coffee." He quickly moves to the next item on his agenda, and keeps his eyes fixated on his laptop, avoiding eye contact with me. The tasteless broth passes the scrutiny.

There is much discussion about when to release the new website to Tenco. Ralf and Ashley keep saying that their code isn't ready for release. Jack states, in a commanding voice, that the website will be released in two weeks precisely. While at the meeting, I remembered that I had neglected to respond to Uncle Miguel's letter. After all, he did say that he was planning to speak to Mr. Trevrel, Juliette, Ophelia and Desdemona on my behalf. I should at least thank him for his efforts and enquire as to how things went. I have been so busy with my plan, ideas swirling inside my brain, that I've forgotten all my social graces.

After the meeting, Ralf and Ashley spend the rest of the day complaining about the deadline.

Ralf: "You can't rush code."

Ashley: "Yeah! Man, this *is* a work of art."

"I always felt I was an artist."

"Yeah!"

"Yeah!"

"I am a code artiste."

"I need inspiration."

" A muse."

"Oh, yes, a new muse."

Will I ever lose the urge to roll my eyes whenever I hear Ashley and Ralf conversing? My resistance to the urge sends my eyes into agitation. With lengthy conversations, I can feel my poor eye sockets throbbing with the desire to orbit a circular motion.

Letter to Uncle Miguel

Dear Uncle Miguel,

Thank you for your kind words in your last letter. You are a constant boost to my spirit. As usual, you provided sage advice from a wise mind. Alas, patience is a challenge for me. Luckily we live in the modern world, where shortcuts can be found where the virtues of patience don't need to tread. I have decided to take your advice with regards to work, at least for now, but I have a surprise up my sleeve. I am not ready to reveal my act of mischief yet, but you will be the first to hear of my plans in the coming months.

I do feel grateful for your intercession on my behalf with dear Juliette, Ophelia and Desdemona. I hope your meeting with them was fruitful and that they have wisely decided to heed your advice. Please let me know of the results and what progress you have made on that front.

I am afraid that in my last letter, I neglected to inquire as to your affairs. How is your work at the presidential palace? No doubt, you have heavy responsibilities that keep you occupied. Thinking about that makes me appreciate your taking the time to help me solve my petty little problems.

I pray that this letter finds you well and that you are enjoying a pleasant spring in our beautiful homeland. Please relay my greetings to the sand, the sky and the birds that fly past fluffy clouds. I find myself yearning for the strangest things now that I have tasted the bitter sand of foreignness.

Nelly Nasah

Washington, D.C.

USA

Blair

I start by breaking into websites and changing subtle things to gain confidence. I change the copyright notice at the bottom of a web page, or the font. Now that I understand the ins and out of Internet hacking, I have to get ready for my first big hit. I need to choose a website that is important so that my work will be noticed, but I don't want my first job to be the most noticeable, either. Also, I need to build a whole new creative design. I can't possibly use my peacock design, since that would be a dead giveaway—Jack, Ralf and Ashley would all recognize the design element and figure out that it was I who had perpetrated the hack attack.

It is during my ride up with Elvi that a woman walks into the elevator holding a potted orchid in her hands. Once again, Elvi provides the answer to my most burning question: the beauty of the flower, the way it shivers in the elevator as if it is afraid of a predator, the richness of the purple color—all of this inspires me to create a website design that is based on orchids. I create a hand-drawn font pretending that I am using stems of orchids to shape letters, but all the lines look forced and rigid. It looks wrong, the way a bodybuilder dancing ballet would vex your senses. As a child, I used to make crowns from dandelions, which I would play with while frolicking in the backyard of our house. I feel a deep urge to buy a large bunch of cut orchids and mold them into shapes and letters. Unfortunately, I have to resist the urge, for there is no way I can possibly make that look like actual work. I must wait until I get home to satisfy my urge; I have no choice but to spend the rest of the day doing Snugoo work.

It is after lunch that Jack calls me into his office. Immediately after I sit down opposite his desk: "Tenco is unhappy with the delays in fixing all the bugs in their website," he declares, while crinkling his nose so it looks like a turtle's neck.

I want to shout, "Hey! I finished the website design ahead of time, and none of this is my fault at all!" but I know how much Jack disapproves of stating the obvious, and so I instead remain silent. Jack then informs me that I have to travel to Seattle the next day to give Tenco a presentation. It is my job to convince them that everything is fine; Ashley and Ralf are busy fixing bugs, and Jack doesn't want either one of them distracted by anything—so it falls upon me to put our client's mind at ease. I want to find an excuse to say no. I need to go buy a bunch of orchids and build the alphabet using them—I am about to make the first hit as Insekab! I wish I could tell Jack that my work on this side of North America is far more important than anything I could achieve in Seattle—nobody will remember a dorky website where people can place orders on sheets of metal; however, the cultural implications of a website design revolution will impact the thoughts and behavior of many generations to come.

"I am not a computer programmer—what if they ask me technical questions?" I protest, hoping to avoid the trip.

"You have attended all of our bug review meetings, and you understand the issues that are involved." The words came out of Jack's mouth in a monotonic voice, so a rolling of the eyes is not necessary. Then Jack remembers something. His voice changes, and he even looks straight at me. "Hey! You remember that ten days ago, you gave Ashley the idea of replacing C# code with JavaScript, and that completely fixed the flickering bug in all our menus. I think you have a knack for this computer programming stuff. You don't even know it. God knows, web design is not your strength!" The last sentence he says while laughing.

Normally I would have minded being mocked, but this was the first time I've ever seen Jack laugh. Seeing his teeth shining through his mouth, his chest rising up and then deflating down in quick succession, is confounding me into silence. I want to shout back, "Why don't you go yourself—it's not like you do anything around here." But I know that Jack enjoys reasonable arguments only when they originate from his own head.

No more reasons to protest arise during the meeting.

At home, I pack a suitcase instead of arranging alphabets using gorgeous orchids.

Jack has arranged a meeting at Tenco's office in Seattle, where I am to give a presentation of our progress. The boardroom has a large, clear glass table surrounded by black leather chairs. I am to convince the Tenco people that everything is going just fine; that the website will be functional in a couple of weeks.

As if the design of the room were not in sufficiently poor taste, everybody at the meeting is drinking coffee out of large paper cups. I try to keep my feeling of revulsion at bay, thinking instead about the flavor of coffee mixed with diluted paper.

These people don't need a demo of the new website; they need a lesson on how to drink coffee from ceramic cups! They need an introduction to the art of enjoying a hot beverage.

In the room, I am introduced to four men: the CEO; the CIO; a marketing representative of one sort or another; and Blair, the resident computer programmer. Given my limited experience with computer programmers—only two, and I wonder whether this computer programmer also has a social impediment—from outward appearances, he seems perfectly normal (for an American, that is). He is wearing a stripped white t-shirt and blue jeans. His sandy brown hair has wild curls unabashedly sprinkled across his head. Hazel green eyes adorn his face, making him look even younger than he probably is—I am guessing that Blair is 22 years old. He is holding a paper cup filled with coffee like all his colleagues, but otherwise he sits silently with a blank expression while I give the demo. He doesn't seem to be suffering from the urge to interrupt every sentence in order to hear his own voice, like Ashley does. In truth, this is only the third time I have given a presentation. The first two were at Snugoo's, with the first a total disaster and the second being a soup broth consumption session. This is totally different. I don't care much about the outcome of the meeting, yet I find my hands shaking with nerves. Trickles of sweat stream from my armpits, making the long journey to between my thighs. Strange how out of balance I feel, given how little investment I have towards my presentation.

After the demo, I display the list of our bugs and show the progress we are making on fixing them, and that is when all the questions come gushing forward like an Amazonian downpour. When will you fix all the bugs? Why is it taking so long? Why are there so many bugs? Why did you use alphaBit graphical components?

To my amazement, I am answering all the questions in a reasonable fashion. It seems that I was paying attention in our team meetings at Snugoo after all, or perhaps all of my research on how to crack a website has filled my head with technical lingo. This is when Blair enquires, "Which part did you develop?"

"I created the website design."

"Why did your company send a website designer and not a programmer to this meeting?"

"All of the computer programmers are busy fixing bugs...."

"Oh! That is disappointing. For a minute, I thought you knew what you were talking about!"

"I do know what I am talking about; I worked on the most important aspect of this website—the part that all the users will interact with."

"But that has nothing to do with engine that runs the site—the meat; nobody cares what the website looks like—only what it does."

"I disagree! I think what it looks like is of the utmost importance. I am certain that if you were attuned to your users, you wouldn't be saying that."

Things are becoming intense in the room. Blair's face flares into red hues that remind me of burning charcoal. He inhales a deep breath, no doubt to gather sufficient strength to hit me with yet another stupid retort that exposes his ignorance about life.

The CIO interjects. "That will be all for the technical assessment, Blair; thank you for your contribution. Let's move on to the updated project plan and rollout plan, please."

I continue with the meeting after drinking a glass of water, which I made sure was served in glass cup and not a paper cup. Blair and I shoot each other looks of animosity that feel like poisoned arrows for the rest of the meeting. It doesn't take me long to figure out what Blair's social impediment is—he is a stupid, arrogant idiot who lacks an understanding of the most basic elements of taste. I guess this proves the theory that all computer programmers are broken human beings in one form or another, although three is not a very representative sample. The lack of any normal human beings in my circle of acquaintance who are also computer programmers does seem to point in that direction, though.

Flame War

When I get back to Washington, D.C., Jack calls me into his office to congratulate me on my successful mission in Seattle. "The Tenco people have agreed to an extension of our deadline, and feel optimistic about the new website." At first, I am happy to be receiving this sentence of praise from Jack—in truth, this is a very rare sentence of praise. It has been a long time since I have impressed anybody.

Then a darker thought occurs to me: "What if this translates to many more of these trips?" More trips only mean more delays in my *real* work.

I am eager to get back to my orchid website design. On my way home from work, I purchase a large bunch of orchids which cost me a pretty penny. I lay the delicate flowers on a large white sheet and begin to shape the letters of the alphabet. Oh, what fun I am having. I feel like an eight-year-old child building sandcastles by the beach. The letters look whimsical; there is a sense of playfulness in their construction, and I fall in love with each letter. I am falling in love with language as if I am discovering it anew. It hits me that I can build the font by taking photographs instead of drawing a stylized version of my hand construction. I go to bed that night filled with happiness as if a source of light is lodged into my bosom and is shooting rays out to all the dark corners of my body.

The next morning, I go to work eager to turn my photographs into a font, making sure to keep Elvi abreast of my progress. Elvi stops on each floor, opens his doors and then closes them, although there is no one there. Elvi is performing a little dance for me to celebrate the joy I feel in my stomach. I appreciate the gesture, and give his wall a heartfelt hug when we finally reach the fourth floor.

At my desk, there is an email from blair.young@tenco.com. "No doubt he is about to congratulate me on my brilliant presentation three days earlier" is my guess.

Subject: Truth

Dear Nelly:

Although you have fooled my bosses with a pretty PowerPoint presentation, dazzling them with lovely pictures and a few nifty features, I want to assure you that you didn't fool me, not for one minute. I will take it upon myself to make sure that they see the inadequate nature of your silly software. Unlike the simple-minded nature of my bosses, I am a real hardcore computer programmer. Nothing speaks the truth like code. A day of reckoning will take place.

No disrespect intended,

Blair

●–○ ●–○ ●–○

Subject: Re: Truth

Dear Blair:

No offence taken. You are free to form any opinion that you please, such as your disregard for website design or your disgust with my effective presentation. The code speaks the truth to your computer programmer eyes. However, my website design speaks the truth to anybody with the gift of eyesight. You may choose to look or keep your eyes closed. That is your choice.

To Free Will,

Nelly

●–○ ●–○ ●–○

Subject: Free Will

Dear Nelly:

Perhaps you think that you are clever by invoking the lofty concept of free will. Since you are from a country where parents drive their children in the trunk of their car in the hopes of sparing them the fate of being shot by snipers, I daresay your stance is insipid, indeed. Even more infuriating is your esteem for website design in general, and your own website design in particular. It is a well-known fact that the Internet would be far better without any website design at all, or perhaps the most minimalist of designs at best. Take the Craigslist website as a case in point. It uses the most minimal of designs that never changes and uses no images, yet it runs on a powerful engine that serves over 20 billion page views in any given month. A billion is one thousand million, just in case your pretty designer head gets confused. Most users, in fact, prefer the simplistic design because it allows them to quickly and efficiently navigate the site without pretty pictures getting in the way. If it weren't for the narrow vision of marketing folks with MBAs who think the Internet is no different than setting up a shoe store, professionals such as myself would design all websites to follow Craigslist's brilliant model.

Glad you were spared the land mines when you immigrated to my country,

Blair

●-o ●-o ●-o

Subject: Re: Free Will

Blair:

Your ignorance astounds me. Had you bothered to learn history, you would have known that I come from a country where four great civilizations have risen at a time when your ancestors were still living in caves. Perhaps you were told that it was your grandfather who invented democracy, free speech and equality. I hate to shock you, given your tender young age, but the truth is that the tooth fairy doesn't exist, and humanity has grappled with high concepts of the human condition for thousands of years. I am sorry if I made you cry, but you were bound to discover the truth one day, anyway. I draw from a civilization that is 4,000 years old; what do you have to back you up? Two hundred dinky years? Oooooooooooh! Eye roll! Pffffft! Excuse me if I fail to pretend that I am impressed.

After you touch upon basic history, I suggest that you give rudimentary geography a try. Do have a glance through a world atlas, will you?. Yes, I know, to you Americans, all countries outside your borders seem the same. They are all those weird places, far away, over there with weird names and strange languages. It might shock you to find out that each one of those colored areas on the world map has a distinct character, culture, language, history and current political climate. I was shocked, too, when I discovered that there was whole world outside my own country, when I was six years of age.

I do hope you were toilet-trained by your mother by now, because that is one subject I don't wish to have to explain in an email. However, I am happy to illuminate all the other recesses of ignorance in your brain.

Cheers;

Nelly

●–o ●–o ●–o

Subject: comedy

Nelly,

I forwarded your email to my roommates. We all studied computer science at the university together. It has been the laughingstock of our shared house for the last 3 days. Rajeev thinks that you must be a very frustrated lady. Jim suspects that perhaps you are not getting along with your therapist, or perhaps you stopped taking your pills. Ryan is wavering between the theory that you have irritable bowel syndrome or suffer from a head concussion. I have contributed a few suggestions of my own. Please, Nelly, do take better care of yourself, whatever it is that you suffer from, even if your condition does provide fantastic comedic respite, no doubt, to multitudes of people. I do wish you a fast recovery.

All the best,

Blair

Most Eloquent of Insults

More insulting than Mr. Darcy's question to Elizabeth in Jane Austen's novel when he asked her, "Could you expect me to rejoice in the inferiority of your connections?— to congratulate myself on the hope of relations, whose condition in life is so decidedly beneath my own?" More eloquent than Faulkner's insult to Hemingway when he referred to him with a few choice words: "He has never been known to use a word that might send a reader to the dictionary." More biting than Mark Twain's remark about a fantasy encounter with Jane Austen: "Every time I read 'Pride and Prejudice,' I want to dig her up and hit her over the skull with her own shin-bone." My next email to Blair is decidedly the most eloquent insult—a work of pure venom. It is oh, so cleverly disguised as an apology and a thank you note. No doubt, Blair will be lulled into a prideful feeling of victory for a few seconds when he initially sees the subject line stating "Thank you for the lesson". I can imagine his hazel eyes getting wider and wider with surprise as he reads the rest. That self-assured smile gets bent like a smashed car as he comes across my final line.

It is about time somebody brought down that arrogant idiot by an inch or two, and I, Nelly, step up to the task. You would be justified to assume that I labored over the email for days and weeks. However, it was a bolt of inspiration that birthed it into existence. I sat down, and the writing flowed vigorously like the Potomac River in Washington, D.C. I wrote the whole letter in a single sitting. When I was finished, I felt a sweet sensation of victory, like little butterflies tingling the bottom of my spine. I imagine Blair pounding his fists on the table, muttering insults of the vulgar kind and even smashing things. The one thing I don't expect is a reply. For what could he possibly come back with? He can't compete with the articulateness of my expression. To send me back a common insult would be to admit defeat and forever declare his intellect a redundant appendage of a brainpower that has already run near to depletion. A letter of insult with greater eloquence is not possible, for my letter is already perfect in that regard.

I wasn't going to include the letter here, but for literary purposes only, I have changed my mind. If you choose to borrow these words, please use them responsibly. This letter is a deadly weapon; inflict only on those who deserve it.

Subject: Thank you for the lesson

Dear Blair:

Back home, we have a saying in our ancient language: "Akbar menak beyoum, afham menak besanah," which translates to "the one who is older than you by a single day understands a year's worth more than you do," implying that older people have more knowledge. Well, I think that saying is nonsense. I have met many older people who didn't know what they were talking about. In fact, I have discovered that it is the younger people from whom we should try to learn our lessons. And you are a case in point. You see, I am a few years older than you, and I have learned so much from you by just meeting you once.

For example, remember how you talked about land mines and snipers with regards to my country of origin? In my old, backwards days, I would have called that an ignorance of facts. But now, thanks to you, I realize that I live with a harsh and judgmental mentality. Thanks to you, I learned that your way is called liberal and creative bending of factual verities, for who cares about current events when all can be mashed up into one?

I did my best to tackle your ignorant comments by sharing my honest views. I assured myself that I was communicating with a mature and reasonable person, and that by doing my side of sharing, I was facilitating a discussion that allowed for depth. By not sharing, I was holding myself in a power position—not allowing you to form your own informed opinion about the matter. When I learned that you had shared my emails with your roommates, I immediately jumped to a conclusion and thought, "What a silly teenager who behaves like he has never talked to a real woman with brains before." But now that I think about it, I realize that I was being very old-fashioned in my ways. This is not immature behavior; this is open-minded, egalitarian sharing of pertinent information.

When you forwarded our entire email conversation to your friends without asking my permission in the matter, the first word that popped into my mind was betrayal. Ah! Once again, I learn a new lesson on how my brain is wired the wrong way. Sharing private emails with others instead of having the decorum to allow me to decide whether I want to discuss my own views on the matter is not a betrayal at all. Decorum is an old fogey word, anyway. It is called enlightened oneness with the natural forces of nature.

To you, respect is the odd sunny day in Seattle; but I grew up in the desert, where it was sunny every day. Every once in a while, a sandstorm would arise and hide the sun behind a yellow haze. During those days, I tasted sand in my mouth and my eyes stung in pain as the sand granules hit my corneas. Doctors prescribed relocation to asthma patients, for only the tough can survive when it is sunny every day. Look how green and beautiful Seattle is. Clearly, your model of the odd sunny day yields better results. After all, what do I know? I am a failure on so many fronts. Next to your varied talents, I can't help but stand in awe of your awesomeness.

In fact, you are so splendidly great, mortal words can't comprehend your utter prominence. I only wish that I would gain a fraction of your sense importance. Here I am, talking to you using your cultural references, dressed in western clothing, and it is I who don't understand your culture. Yet you have been able to thoroughly understand my country of origin and declare yourself an expert in its history without any effort all. You don't know a single fact about my country, you never heard the name of any poet from my homeland, and you can't stand to listening to one minute of our music; nevertheless, you can expertly analyze my behavior with reference to the disturbed images you have seen in TV. Dude! You are incredible. One day, I will be able to do that and forgo the burden of study.

So thank you for the valuable lesson. I can't wait for my next one.

I wish you happy hand-induced sperm liberation while you write email sermons on freedom of speech and democracy while you view released from clothing images. You seem to be good ... at doing all three together, I mean.

Tell all your friends that Nelly sends them her best wishes for a tender and sweet infiltration up their rears.

Sincerely;

Nelly

Now isn't that good? That is great! I only wish that I could post that letter somewhere public, so that everybody in the world could behold its greatness.

One useful thing came out of my flame war with Blair: I no longer need to think about which website to hack into. The answer is now as obvious as the sun: Insekab' s first hit will be Craigslist, killing two birds with one stone—rubbing more salt into Blair's injury; proving to the whole world that a good design can improve all websites. Perhaps one day, I will send Blair an actual thank you letter.

First Hit

I walk into Elvi, telling him everything all at once in jumbled sentences that contain my excitement but not my meaning. When our ride together is over, I rub his wall with the palm of my hand and tell him, "I am so happy because I am about to conquer the world." Elvi looks peaceful and quiet; I can sense that he is delighted for me. At work, I attack the task like a hungry hammerhead shark about to devour a diver. Finishing my orchid design is an urgent priority. I imagine all the poor billions who use Craigslist shrieking with pleasure at the relief from the plain sameness they have endured for years. I create a set of page designs where a single stem of orchid sprouts from different sides. On one page the sprout appears on the top, the second on the lower left, and so on. At the bottom of each page, I make sure to include "hacked by Insekab". With my new font and my creative website design, I am ready to finally do what I have been dreaming about for two months. One last detail remains—to figure out how to hack into the Craigslist website.

Ashley shows up at 10:00 a.m. and yells out loud, "I am in bug rut!" Once he ascertains that he has everybody's attention, he continues with a rant about how he has been fixing bugs for weeks on end and that he wishes to start developing something new.

"I don't mean to state the obvious, but you need to make this software work before you move on to the next thing." Am I stating the obvious?

He looks back at me as if I had made the most heinous of statements. Then he proceeds to tell me the story of how he was in charge of an entire software department in Thailand at one point and had more than forty developers reporting to him. He only troubled himself developing interesting stuff, giving the boring bug fixing to his staff.

"You don't know how tedious this is to a brilliant mind such as myself," he bellyaches liked a child resisting cleaning his room. You might think the bug fixing was killing him. At last! He settles into his chair and begins to stare at his computer monitor.

I am happy to regain enough equanimity so as to resume my critical mission.

It takes me three whole days to figure out how to break into Craigslist's website. Since all of their software is house-rolled, the known patterns don't work. I had to spend lots of time poking around to understand how it functioned. I even posted a fake advertisement on the website to help me get into its brains. Under the Lost and Found section, I posted:

Lost Nightmare

I lost a horrific recurrent nightmare about a white serpent. Gone and vanished overnight, right after I decided to follow a critical purpose in life. If found, please keep it. I don't miss it, nor the serpent. Not. One. Bit!

I laugh loudly as I examine the post on the website. It is the first time in a long time I remember my awful nightmare. I am giggling at the funny advertisement, wondering what people will make of it. I am that happy my sound sleeping has returned since my arrival in Washington, D.C. Oh, how wonderful it is to wake in the morning feeling rested and looking forward to my prized ride with Elvi—and then to proceed to fulfill a useful purpose in life! Ralf notices me laughing, and walks over to my desk. "What are you laughing about? Is it some funny cat video on YouTube?" he quizzes me with a raised eyebrow that looks like a skunk's tail.

"Oh! It is nothing; I just remembered something that happened earlier." I close my web browser in a hurry, attempting to hide my fake advertisement on Craigslist. "I am in need of a laugh. The last few weeks have been trying."

At that point, Ashley bangs his desk with his fist and shouts frantically, "Who deleted the database build from two days ago?" There is no answer. Electric silence hangs in the air. He yells louder and louder, "I can't find the database backup from two days ago—who deleted it?" There is still no answer. Ralf and I look at each other, and we both shrug our shoulders. "I have been working massive overtime, fixing bugs from hell, and somebody just went ahead and deleted all my work that I slaved over for the last two days. When I find out who did this, I will suffocate him with my own hands!" He proceeds to slap his desk with his fist. His eyes turn red as if he were about to cry, and then he runs out of the office while yelling," I can't take this anymore!"

Ralf and I exchange a silent moment. "He seems very upset," I say finally, just to break the silence because I don't know what else to say.

"I will go after him and try to calm him down," says Ralf as he runs out of the office.

Jack opens the door of his office and walks out towards me—a rare occurrence. "Did Ashley have another emotional outburst?" He addresses me because I am the only one left sitting there.

"I don't know what happened—he seemed very upset, and then he ran out," I explain. I was saying nothing useful. "When a woman has an emotional outburst, everybody says, 'Women can't handle the stress of the workplace.' Had I behaved like that, that would be the consensus. Somehow, when a man has an outburst in the workplace, everybody feels sympathy for him." The words came out of my mouth like a river flow. My sympathy towards Ashley quickly turns into impatience and even judgment.

Jack sighs quietly while turning his back to me, and walks back into his office, closing the door behind him.

Ralf runs back into the office after two hours. "Don't worry—he will be fine. He is under lots of stress, but I managed to calm him down." Ralf breaths heavily as if he is announcing news of great urgency. Then he sits down to write an email to Jack, to explain that Ashley will take the rest of the day off to rest, and will be back to work tomorrow.

I feel annoyed. All this drama is distracting me from making my first hit.

Impact

The sun is shining as I wake up this morning. I feel impatient to go to work to make my first impact on the Internet world. Finally, everything is in place. I have my design polished and ready. I have figured out how to hack into my target website. On a beautiful day such as today, I prefer to walk to work. I spend lengthy periods of time looking at the sky, observing the shapes of clouds, imagining the reaction of my new design on the world. I can imagine the awed faces of hundreds, thousands, millions of people. No doubt, the relief from the drab design alone will send numerous patrons of Craigslist into pangs of rapture. This will create an avalanche of letters demanding better standards of design to be upheld at Craigslist, and who knows? Perhaps other websites will feel the pressure to do the same.

Elvi greets me with a fresh sparkle. He is glittering all over as if he has been recently polished. Holding his brass rail, I assure him that our day of victory is near.

At my desk, I go straight to work. Placing the new design takes about an hour. The website looks even more beautiful than I had imagined. I have to enlarge all the font sizes to show my unique custom-made font in the best of light. I close my eyes and try to save the feeling of happiness into my memory like a treasure in an oak chest. For the rest of my life, whenever I have a dark day, I can always retrieve this treasure and shine a bright light in any corner that requires it.

Ashley walks in. I quickly close all the open web browsers on my desktop. I would hate for anybody to have an inkling of suspicion towards me. Sitting at his desk, Ashley doesn't even say good morning. While he busies himself staring at his computer monitor, an eerie silence hangs in the air the way fog probably hung in my neighborhood of current residence, giving it its name. Should I approach Ashley and ask him how he is doing? Or should I leave him to his silence?

I am bursting with enthusiasm at my first hit this morning. Thank God I have Elvi to talk to about my victories; otherwise, I would have nobody to share with. I can't tell Ashley or Ralf of my adventures, because I don't trust them to not report me to the authorities. Writing letters about this to my friends in Quari-ay-eh-ay is pointless. Although they understand what websites are, they have probably never heard of Craigslist, and wouldn't be able to understand the great significance of my work.

Ralf finally arrives. He breaks the silence by greeting everybody with a smile. From their chitchat, I gather that it is Jack who had moved the backup database build to a different directory, in his constant urge for order in our filing system. When Ashley didn't find it in the usual place, he assumed that it had been deleted. Once this misconception was clarified, Ashley was able to restore all his work.

"He is not a computer programmer; I don't think he should have access to the source code, anyway," states Ashley emphatically but in a hushed tone. "Oh, well—he is the boss—nothing I can do about it," he continues.

"You look happy today," Ashley remarks as he gets up and walks over to my desk.

"Oh, yes—I am very happy!"

"Perhaps there is a handsome young man on the horizon who has placed that smile on your face?" Ashley's eyes fixate on me to glean any involuntary body language that would betray my secret.

"Nothing like that," I laugh dismissively. "I just had a glorious walk in the sunshine this morning, and I felt like a million dollars by the time I arrived at the office."

"I am glad you are happy. I wish I could say the same about myself. Yesterday I found out from my ex-wife that my eldest daughter has anorexia."

"What is anorexia?" I regret my impulse to discover new things seconds after I utter the question. After all, these days, you can find out everything using Google—no need to betray my ignorance.

"You honestly have never heard of it before?"

"I guess people don't get it in Quari-ay-eh-ay."

"Anorexia is a psychological illness, an eating disorder, where the sufferer has a distorted body image that leads them to excessive weight loss. My daughter was caught posting on a pro-ana forum."

I caught myself before my impulse got the best of me, and I managed not to ask, "What is a pro-ana forum?"

Perhaps Ashley notices the quizzical look on my face and surmises my question. "Pro-ana sites are websites that promote anorexia as a lifestyle choice and encourage kids to stick to it."

"So what do these websites promote?"

"For example, how to suppress their appetite or how to fool their parents into thinking that they are eating when they are not."

This struck me as hilarious.

"So what? They encourage young people to starve and die." I can't stop myself from laughing at such a thought.

Ralf looks annoyed. "An eating disorder is a serious thing, Nelly. Try to be more sensitive," he admonishes me as if I am a child caught torturing a little kitten. I decide not to respond to him, but I don't stop laughing. When I resume a more somber demeanor, Ashley continues with the story about his daughter.

"It must be hard for her. Her mother was a fashion model. Eighteen years ago, a picture of her in a bikini was plastered on the biggest billboard in London, in Trafalgar square. It's a big deal. Major big deal. Imagine any poor girl feeling the pressure of competing against that. I read what my daughter wrote on the forum. She was talking about how much she hated her body. There was so much self-loathing. It just broke my heart...."

I can't believe that I had been uncomfortable in the eerie silence earlier and had wished that Ashley would say something in order to break the ice. I can imagine black crows flying out of his mouth, each one squawking away, filling the room with cries of anguish. I try to focus on my newly-acquired treasure that is stored inside my mind. Restoring the moment gives me great comfort.

After lunch, I hear Ralf squeal with surprise.

"Woooh! Listen to this, you guys—somebody hacked into Craigslist! I just read about it on Slashdot."

"What? When?"

"This morning! They didn't steal anything—didn't even access their database. The only thing that was changed was their website design."

"Look at that ugly website design with flowers," Ashley laughs.

"It is not a flower—it is an orchid," I chime in to correct him.

"This is too funny—clearly a brilliant mind with a great sense of humor." Ralf joins the laughter.

"Or maybe it is an environmentalist who wants us to embrace Mother Earth." Ashley is dripping with sarcasm.

"I love this. Nothing fun has happened on the Internet for the last eighteen months, not since Fark started the extra floppy boobies section." Ralf is now swaying back and forth as he laughs with his whole body.

"Look at that font!" Ashley shrieks with delight. "It looks like a five-year-old girl created it."

I don't mind their stupid and ignorant comments. I wasn't expecting anything better from these two imbeciles.

Fallback

At night I walk back to my apartment, feeling that I am hopping across the clouds in the sky like an angel. Fresh-faced university students are milling about, returning from a long day of studying at Georgetown University. I want to hug every single person I meet. I want to declare at the top of my voice, "I did it! I did it!" The thought extends my smile even wider. At home, I make myself a dinner of pasta decorated with olives, red pepper shreds and artichoke hearts—a simple yet hearty meal. Then I sit down to watch some TV. To my utter surprise, the evening news has coverage of Insekab.

My delight turns into horror when I hear the comments. The news reporter reads:

> Today, Craigslist, the online classified advertisement website used by millions, was hacked by a prankster. The hacker or hackers, referring to themselves as "Insekab," left the website untouched except for altering the website design. Craigslist headquarters noticed something was afoul when they began to receive an avalanche of emails complaining about the elaborate new website design. Initial users of the website thought

that the new website had been designed by Craigslist. Staff of Craigslist were able to restore the old design after 12 hours. The website never ceased to function as usual.

Then there are interviews with different people about their impressions. Here is some of the feedback:

"It was so funny, I wish Insekab had done this on April Fool's—it would have been funnier!"

"This Insekab dude put lots of effort to play a prank on all of us, well done buddy, you rock!"

"Why pick on Craigslist? Why not pick on some evil organization like Microsoft?"

"I kept checking Craigslist the whole day—it gave me continual LOL's that turned into a laughing fit, I am calling it c loooooool list."

The news report goes on:

A spokesperson for Craigslist apologized to all the users of the website, and assured everyone that no private or personal information had been accessed by the hacker. New security measures have been placed to avoid a similar incident in the future.

There are so many things wrong with that news report. This is not a prank, nor a joke! This is a serious web design that I had hoped people would fall in love with. I had fully expected Craigslist to keep it, and appreciate the fact that it had been donated for free. And why do so many people assume that Insekab is a man? Is it too hard to imagine that a woman could do brilliant work?

Waves of sadness come one after the other in rapid succession until I feel overwhelmed. I give in to the tidal wave and cry myself to sleep.

The next morning, I stand inside Elvi's bosom, silent and motionless. I don't know what to tell him. How to explain that our victory is turned into a mockery. At my desk, I look up all the news reactions on the Craigslist hacking. There are news reports from all over the world—not just the U.S.—blog posts, tweets and Facebook discussions. Somebody has started tweeting as Insekab. The Insekab hash tag is trending on twitter. This is pure madness.

#insekab is the modern day banksy

stop commercialism is what #insekab is saying and I support his stand

against fascism and with #insekab

thank you for making me laugh #insekab

#insekab is trying to tell us to go smell flowers and stop browsing the internet

#insekab is telling us to play with orchids, don't take life too seriously. I totally agree with him.

stop hating on #insekab, he is just a clown

I didn't know what fascism is, nor who Banksy is. I look both things up on Google. I want to yell and scream, "No!" I am not making any political statements; I am not making any lifestyle statements; I am not pro nor against any of the things that are mentioned. I am not a man. I was not trying to amuse anybody or make anybody laugh. All the reactions are wrong, wrong and wrong. Everybody is misunderstanding. I wanted to create an object of beauty that would inspire people into creating more beautiful websites.

How I wish I could smack my desk like Ashley did two days ago, and run out of the office in near tears. Gathering all my strength, I walk calmly into the ladies' washroom, which, thankfully, is empty. I wash my face in an attempt to hold back tears. Somehow I find a way to compose myself. I get through my workday pretending that everything is normal.

Ralf and Ashley have yet another one of their stupid dialogues that I try hard not to listen to.

"I wish I was Insekab—I would be feeling mighty high and proud right now!"

"Nah! His design is dandy, but I would have done something much cooler and made a more powerful statement."

"The dandiness is the point of his design; he is calling us all pussies."

"Aaaah! I hadn't thought about it that way. I am beginning to dig it."

"He is telling us to man up."

"Exactly!"

"Like in the old days, when computer programmers owned this space."

"Back when management had no clue what we did, and so we did whatever we wanted."

"Yeah!"

"Double yeah!"

"I wish I could meet this guy!"

"He would be fun to hang out with!"

"I bet he appreciates the ladies like we do."

"He must get lots of pussy for his manliness."

You have no idea how my eye sockets ache at this point. Leave it to Ashley and Ralf to come up with the stupidest conclusions about Insekab.

I am attacked by loneliness the way a heart surgeon opens the chest cavity of a patient: Calmly, methodically and scientifically, but violently, nevertheless. The anesthesia has mercifully made the pain go away. A polite awareness of many months of pain to come is infused in the air. There is nobody to talk to about my state of distress. I remember that I haven't received any letters from Quari-ay-eh-ay for a long time. I guess when there are no problems for me to solve, there is no reason for any of them to write to me. How I wish I would get a letter from somebody—anybody! Or have a problem to busy myself solving. Even a package from Mr. Trevrel, asking to make more handmade bookmarks, would be a comfort.

Eggplant

Three weeks after I sent my triumphant letter, the unexpected happened: Blair sent me a reply. His email stated:

Greetings Nelly,

I have read and re-read your email about 10 times. I haven't been able to sleep for the last two nights. I have been walking around with my head lowered, walking around with a heavy heart. Feeling no desire to work or even to play video games, I am a lost soul with no purpose. I realize now how what I used to consider well-meaning advice, comes across as pontification. I have been reflecting on all past friendships and relationships in my life with new clarity. Am I really that arrogant? ... I must be. Apologies for my behavior. I will cease all email correspondence while I contemplate the source of my egotism.

Regards,

Blair

I feel little butterflies abandoning my lower spine, flying together in formation away from me towards the sun. Instead, there are now pebbles in my stomach, contributing to a heavy feeling in my lower body. Argh! I should be happy. I liberated somebody from his arrogance. This might improve his future relationships, friendships and maybe even his career. One day, Blair might thank me for helping him see the error of his ways. So why do I feel so dreadful?

At night, I toss and turn in my bed. I keep thinking about poor Blair contemplating his life, not able to get pleasure even from playing his darned Halo.

The next day, I go to work and find myself staring into the void. I let out three long labored sighs. The pebbles in my stomach swoosh around, making little clicking sounds as they bounce against each other. Perhaps I am feeling guilt at hurting Blair's feelings. So now I have a new task: To rid myself of the guilty feeling. I can't write an apology letter, since I am not actually sorry for what I have done. Plus, I can't cure with what has caused the disease. I used my noblest eloquence to write the email that has caused the injury; I can't use the same power to write an antidote. A letter of any less eloquence might come across as insincere. Now that I have established myself as the queen of words, a letter of mediocre caliber will be interpreted as off the cuff. I have to find a way to express my emotions through means other than words. A new challenge, indeed. How do I cheer Blair up and express gentle sympathy with his predicament, without seeming as if I were apologizing?

During the lunch hour, I walk around the shopping area surrounding the office. I stroll into a red brick alleyway that I've never been into before. I am staring at the window display of a pen shop. That is when an idea drops from the sky to hit me over the head: "Buy Blair a gift—buy him a pen from this store." As soon as the idea swirls in the maze that is my brain, I can feel the load in my stomach get lighter, and so I know that I am on the right track.

I walk into the pen shop to inspect carefully all of the glass display cases along three walls of the store. A tall, slim man in his mid-thirties approaches me, speaking in a hushed yet forceful tone: "Is there something special that you are looking for today?"

I tell him that I am looking for a birthday gift for a friend. I am too embarrassed to tell him that I am looking for a reconciliation gift for an arrogant young man whom the universe has decided to assign me the unfortunate task of humbling.

The store attendant recommends a sterling silver ballpoint pen with subtle line incisions going lengthwise.

"This is very popular among young gentlemen," he says while handing me the pen with a regal swoop of the arm, as if he were handing me a samurai sword.

It does look manly and elegant in a simple way. I especially like the slimness of the pen. However, something about it doesn't feel right. I hand back the pen, balancing it in both palms of my hand (indicating an appreciation for the opportunity to touch such a prized object). I proceed to look some more across the display case, when my eyes fall on the perfect pen. It is a deep brown, purpley ballpoint with herringbone etching all around. The clip and tips of this pen are trimmed with silver. The pen is handed to me with lesser ceremony; I can sense that the sales attendant disapproves of my choice. However, in my gut, I know that it is the right gift for Blair. I offer the store attendant a most radiant smile that he isn't able to resist, and his scowl quickly relaxes into a natural position for his lips. I present him with my Visa card, and he proceeds to polish the pen with a felt cloth before he places it in a satin-lined gift box.

Later that night, I start writing a gift note by drawing the outline of an eggplant, and then writing:

Dear Blair,

Eggplant is my favorite vegetable. I love roasted eggplant and fried eggplant, but most of all, I love to make baba ghanoush with eggplant, which I decorate with something inspired by Michelangelo. This is exactly what I would be doing right now if I were living somewhere in Seattle. I wish I could give you a proper decorated plate of Quari baba ghanoush to help comfort you in your vulnerable time. One of my favorite things about eggplant is the dark purple-brown color it possesses. It is dark and mysterious; yet, if you contemplate it long enough, you can see that it is also an earthy and comforting color. Darker than black but gentler than grey. To me, eggplants symbolize male energy. At times they are bitter and they have a strong taste; yet when cooked properly at the hands of a master chef, their inner sweetness can overwhelm everything else. Unfortunately, I can't send you an eggplant by mail; however, here is the next best thing: A ballpoint pen in eggplant color. I hope you can accept this gift as a small token of my friendship.

Best regards,

Nelly

Three weeks later, I receive a box in the mail. Inside is a red stapler. It comes with a note that is written over a drawing of a bell pepper:

Dear Nelly,

Red pepper is my favorite vegetable. I love the taste of roasted red peppers, sautéed red peppers and even uncooked red peppers. I don't think that there is a single thing that you can do to a red pepper that could possibly ruin it. In my mind, red peppers symbolize feminine energy. They taste great straight off the vine. Any average person can improve on them by just applying a little bit of heat—no culinary skills are required at all. The taste is my favorite part; however, the color is a delight to the eyes. I wish I could mail you a box of red peppers. Since I am worried that they might spoil along the way, I decided to instead send you the next best thing—a stapler in the color of a red pepper. It might aid you in organizing your papers and artistic creations. Try to avoid pricking your finger on the sharp tips, lest you injure yourself and go into a deep stupor like Snow White did. Your gift and the sentiment behind it are accepted.

Regards,

Blair

Now I feel confused. On the one hand, it seems that he is accepting my gift; but on the other hand, he is calling me Snow White. Does this mean that he thinks I am a spoiled princess? A pen is a much finer gift than a stapler, anyway.

I take the stapler with me to the office. It looks mighty pretty sitting on my desk at Snugoo. Whenever I look at it, it makes me think of red peppers, and I start craving them.

Red peppers do look beautiful on their own—all that rich color would be spoiled if you added decorations to it. I have finally found a food that I can purchase without feeling the need to decorate. It is such a relief! I now eat red peppers twice a week. And Blair's stapler is beautiful on its own. I had thought about decorating it with rhinestones and feathers, but somehow the decoration would break the richness of the solid color. This is the first time I find myself appreciating plain solid color. Oh, no—am I being influenced by my surroundings? Or is this an evolvement in my taste? Hard to tell.

No Straight Lines

At work, Ashley and Ralf are working hard on meeting the new deadline. Each one sits at his desk staring at his monitor, forgoing the silly jibber jabber in which they both usually engage. How I wish there were this peace and quiet in the office when I have important work to focus on. Instead, this new silence is annoying: I have nothing to do at work right now. I have only minor corrections in the website design for Tenco, which take me only about 30 minutes each day. As for my real work, the response to my first hit is so bewildering, I need to take time to think about it and process it before I proceed with any new projects. I almost wish that Ashley would tell me one of his obnoxious stories about his life, just so that I could pass the time at work.

I have consulted with Elvi about my dilemma, but for the first time in our friendship, he is silent—no response of any sort and no advice that I am able to discern. Perhaps I am just not picking up on his signals, or perhaps he just doesn't know what to say.

I still have to come to the office during regular office hours, just in case I am required to make any minor adjustments to the design.

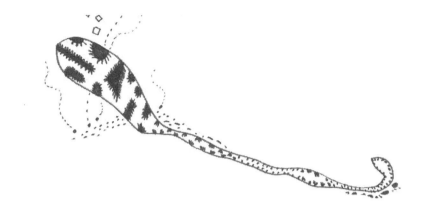

I sit at my desk most of the day, staring into the void and attempting to answer the question, "What does it all mean?" I can't believe that my work has been compared to that of Banksy. Although I am a great fan of stencil, his designs lack the refinement to which I aspire. I have done some online research on his graffiti work in England and other cities of the world; the only one with any merit is the one he did on the separation wall in Bethlehem, Palestine. His drawing looks like a crack in the wall that opens up into the seashore and trees. It is both beautiful and funny in an ironic way. I do get that one. But all the rest of his drawings are about substance, while neglecting the elements of style. Poor judgment on his part, if you ask me!

Since our styles are so categorically different—well! I have style, and he doesn't; I fail to see any basis for comparison. I suppose the similarity is that both of us do our work without first asking for permission. But that is where the resemblance ends. I mean, Banksy stencils rats all over the place. How crass is that? Very few people thought that my orchid design was beautiful or inspirational, and most took it as a joke or a statement indicating political or social critique. I think I am beginning to see what is wrong with this civilization: people are unable to accept anything at face value. Everything is looked at through yellow shades of irony. How to get people to simply look and see exactly what tis there, without anticipating the opposite lurking in a corner somewhere?

The more I think about it, the more I suspect that people who loved the design are afraid to come out and say so in public, because they are afraid of looking like fools. A natural reaction in a place where good taste is held hostage by the whims of the dictatorship of the unrefined and crass is the only thing that is acceptable. There has to be a way to reach these people and create a safe space for them in which to voice their opinion. I need to think of a better design, a more powerful design— something that is so heart-wrenchingly beautiful that it becomes sarcasm-proof.

O God! This mission is even harder than I had anticipated. Now that I have an understanding of the malady affecting the people in this country, I think I can come up with a good cure.

The realization of a new task cheers me up, but the silence in the office still bothers me. I am feeling homesick in new ways that I can't explain—like a carpet that is threadbare, remembering a long-gone glory.

All over Washington, D.C., cherry blossoms are blooming, covering the city in pink and white clouds that hover over people's heads. It is explosively beautiful.

As I walk to and from work, I ignore the ugly architecture of the city, because my attention is focused on absorbing the exquisiteness of the cherry blossoms. Who knew that a tree that looks so bare and ordinary could surprise with eloquent displays of color. But instead of feeling happiness or pleasure at all this, it instead evokes feelings of loneliness and sadness. I remember the streets of Quari-ay-eh-ay lined with perfectly designed buildings. My friends, and all their silliness. And how I miss my dear Uncle Miguel. I wish I could wrap my arms around him. Even Mr. Trevrel, with his modern ideas and strange obsessions—at least I had good conversations with him. I was always able to tell him what was on my mind. There haven't been any letters from home in months, and now that I had sort of made a request to be left alone, I don't know how to resume the conversation. I wish I could find some ruse, some compelling reason to initiate a conversation with all of these people. I could always forgo letter writing and send gifts. That would at least initiate a "thank you" note which would later provoke a letter. Now I have two tasks on my mind—building a heartachingly beautiful irony-proof website design, and buying perfect gifts for Uncle Miguel, Juliette, Desdemona, Ophelia and Mr. Trevrel. Both tasks require careful planning and immaculate execution.

The silence at work is pounding inside my head like a hammer drill. I hear Ralf's heavy breathing when he comes to the office. Ashley's loud munching during lunchtime is even more audible. Then there are all the quiet little grunts, hums and haws. Both of them are creating a soundtrack to their thoughts while busy with their work. I never thought I would be wishing for Ralf and Ashley to resume their regular yammering. What is even worse, the silence is reminding me of all the horrid stories that Ashley has told me over the last eight months—the anorexic daughter, the fall from an airplane, the languished stay in a Turkish hospital, his trauma at losing his Yahoo account—all of it is coming back into my imagination in full Technicolor detail that is exponentially more disturbing than the original telling. I am yearning to hear one of Ashley's stories, if only to relieve my imagination of the burden of his old stories. Surely the worst of his stories has been told, and only more acceptable stories remain! How many heartbreaking, dark tales can a single person possess?

To my own surprise I get up from my chair, and for the first time, I approach Ashley's desk to initiate a conversation. The astonishment is clear on Ashley's face. Ralf stares in our direction. My mouth goes dry and my mind is blank. I should have planned a conversation opener before getting up.

Blurting out the first thing that pops in my head, I say, "Hey, Ashley! How is your daughter doing?"

"Much better; thank you for asking. My ex-wife tells me that she is seeing a doctor and responding well to the treatment. Now it is my son who is in trouble. Yesterday his mom caught him in the washroom. His eyes were bloodshot and he was very sick—the poor fellow. He tried marijuana for the first time ever and became sick as a dog afterwards. My ex called me, in absolute hysterics. I told her the boy is 14 years old and will try the stuff one day anyway. I told her not to worry. The fact that it made him sick is a good thing—he is less likely to try it again. Have you tried marijuana before? I can't stand the smell of it. I don't mind heroin or ecstasy, but marijuana—yuck! I think I am allergic to it. The best trip I had was with meth. I would take meth everyday if it wasn't so darned addictive. Meth transports me into a world where there are no straight lines. Cars ripple around in loops, streets coil back and forth like snakes, and every surface is a wave that rises and falls with reckless abandon. At first it might seem that existing in that world would be easy, but it takes lots of work. Every time you take a step, you have no idea where the Earth will meet your foot, so you have to jump and hope that something will appear to catch you. If I had a penny for each time I fell on my face in that world, I would be a millionaire in this world. Money has no meaning in that world, because you can never hold on to it. Whenever you grab a dollar out of your pocket, it just flies out of your fingers and turns into a red balloon. The only thing that is the same here as there are the birds. Because they are able to fly through a shaky place with precision and not be affected by the general wobbliness, they are at the top of the food chain. So watch out for the birds in the shaky, no-straight-line world. They will swoop down and peck out your eyes if they get the opportunity. My best friend in the shaky, no-straight-line world is the wall clock. It mysteriously always points in exactly the right direction that I should be going. I haven't visited there for a long, long time after having had one particularly bad experience...."

After one full hour of hearing about the shaky, no-straight-line world, I fluctuate between agitation and mental anguish. "Why on Earth did I engage Ashley in a conversation?" The question buzzes around, making the infinity shape over my head. "What next? Perhaps I should ask Ralf out on a date?" All the hysteria in the world could not make me stoop to such a low. "Not even in shaky, no-straight-line world could that happen!"

After lunch, Ralf approaches my desk, no doubt encouraged by my conversation with Ashley, and makes an attempt at small talk.

"So what are your plans for the weekend?"

"I don't know; I haven't made any plans yet."

"There is a new exhibit at the Smithsonian called "The Art of Video Games." It tracks the development of video games over 40 years. I found it interesting, especially in that I actually played most of the games they have on display. Reminded me of my childhood."

"I am not interested in video games, but perhaps they have other exhibits at the Smithsonian that I would be interested in—do they have other exhibits?"

"Are you telling me that you haven't been to the Smithsonian yet?" Ralf's eyebrows are both raised, like two grey bushes.

"No—is it worth a visit?"

Ralf snorts twice as if he is experiencing a private visit into shaky, no-straight-line world.

"Which planet are you from? The Smithsonian is the finest, grandest set of museums and art galleries in the whole entire world. People come to Washington, D.C., from all over the country—no—from all over the world, just to visit it. You have been living here for a year!"

"Actually, only eight months."

"Whatever! Don't you live in Foggy Bottom?"

"Yes."

"You are walking distance from the Smithsonian. You just have to go over there, and the sooner the better. The best part is that everything is free—no admission fees."

"I have seen advertising by the Smithsonian in the underground metro station—they always have interesting pictures. I guess that's what I will do this weekend."

"I still don't understand why you haven't gone there in all this time."

"I have been busy."

"With what?"

"Work!"

"Work is only five days a week and 9-5—what do you do the rest of the time?"

"I think about my work."

Naturally, I allowed Ralf to get confused and think that I was talking about my work at Snugoo; I can't tell him that I have far more critical work on my plate.

Ralf shakes his head in disbelief while walking back to his desk. His reaction amuses me. I am glad that to the likes of Ralf, I appear to be an alien creature. However, his suggestion does seem interesting. I have been through many trials and tribulations in the last two months, and have been working tirelessly, with no breaks. I have been my own slave driver. An excursion involving a few fresh sights might refill the creative well and recharge my brain's batteries. My mind is made up— this weekend will be dedicated to exploring the Smithsonian.

Salt

Elvi's silence is driving me to desperation. Is he mad at me? Or is he going through something of his own that is making him feel morose. If only I knew what or who had offended my darling friend, I would do whatever it takes to lighten his burden. I need to go into the office building at 10:00p.m. and have a lengthy confrontation with Elvi—my recent brief encounters with Elvi are getting in the way of having a deeper conversation. I need to be able to talk to him for as long as it takes, without interruptions by others in the building. I bring a flashlight in case the building is dark in the evening. I have never been in the office this late, and I don't know what to expect.

I stand inside Elvi and press the emergency stop button. I hold his brass railing in silence for five minutes.

Look! I don't know why you stopped talking to me, but whatever it is, I am sorry. I am certain that we can work it out.

Silence.

Look, Elvi, I am not leaving here until you start talking to me. I've got all night long. I don't need to sleep. The white snake dream gave me fantastic sleep deprivation training. I can last without sleep for months! Don't challenge me; you know how strong-willed I am.

Still no reaction from Elvi.

I wait for 15 minutes, my hands crossed, and then I push the button for the fourth floor, where I fetch a chair from Snugoo's office and place it inside Elvi.

Look, Elvi, I am coming inside to see an intimate you ... okay! There is nothing you can do to stop me.

I stand on top of the chair and access the elevator shaft by pushing out the trap door at the top of the elevator car. The door swings out, releasing several decades' worth of dust, which flies in the air around me like confetti. I try to suppress a cough by placing a hand over my mouth. It is like instructing a pregnant woman in her ninth month to hold it in and not give birth—useless. My eyes are irritated and my nose is drippy. An avalanche of coughing follows. How I wish I had brought a surgical mask. I can feel my heart pounding; I have never done anything so daring before.

I lift my hands up, grip the edge of the trap door and pull myself through into the shaft well. I kneel on top of the car, waiting to regain my balance. I steady my breath and reach for the flashlight in my back pocket. The car sways from side to side, producing booming sounds from the car's walls hitting the edges of the shaft. It sounds like something from a horror movie right before the hero is about to encounter his nemesis for the first time. My flashlight is capturing dust particles as if it were a magnet attracting iron dust. Metal wrapped in grease and grime, cables, pulleys, harsh edges—I am gazing at the innards of a powerful beast.

"Wow!" I gasp. "It is all so beautiful!" The contrast with the inside of the elevator car couldn't be more striking; yet, seeing this side of Elvi makes me admire him that much more. "You keep an immaculate front, yet perform a gargantuan task of heavy lifting every day. Insipid are most of your interactions with the people who use your services every day. You are my hero, Elvi; I wish I were more like you. I can see you. I can really, really see."

"Since you will not talk to me, I will tell you a story. This is an old fairy tale from the Czech Republic that my father told me when I was 19. I don't know how this story is told in its country of origin; I only know the version that my father told me. Here it is.

"People say that stories contain universal truths. Nah! I don't buy it. The truth doesn't make up stories; people do. Do you think that thieves, crooks and murderers don't know how to spin a yarn? Why, people like that tell the best tales. Every story has several sides, and then there is the truth. You can chase your tale until you are dizzy from untangling all the arcs in the geometry of a narrative. But in the end, you will end up writing one of those dry academic papers that nobody reads, yet it holds claim over factuality. Nobody wants to know the truth. People want to hear a simple story: beginning, middle and end, with an interesting twist for a conclusion. In the end, none of the sides—not even the truth—matter. What really matters is what you chose to tell. History is written by those who won the war. Individuals with things to do and places to see don't have time tell each other stories. Every storyteller is either desperate or insane, and sometimes both.

"Once upon a time, in magical lands, long before science spoiled things by explaining it away, lived a king who presided over a glorious kingdom. A bushy beard and grey hair made him look mighty regal. The king had three daughters who were coming of age. He loved them more than he loved life itself. His eldest daughter enjoyed jewelry and fine fashion. Every morning she lined up her maids to carefully choose the perfect ensemble for the day. It was a team effort, matching hair ribbons to shoes. Accessories to the skirt lace. Hairdo to the hand drawn pattern on a fan held in the hand. She always looked like harmony in perfection. By the time she had made her way to the royal court, she was sure to create a once-in-a-lifetime performance with her quiet presence.

"Music and singing were the passion of the second daughter. She played the harp and was so obsessed with tunes and rhythms that instead of talking, she simply sang. Whenever somebody asked her a question, she would answer with a song. She would arrive at the royal court singing, 'Good morning, good morning, I feel so happy right now, good morning, good morning ... all together now....' Her eldest sister tried hard not to roll her eyes. Court advisers thought that such behavior was unbecoming of a princess. The king found it charming, and would wave his hand in dismissal. 'Nah! It is just a phase; she will grow out of it!'

"The third daughter, whose name was Marushka, was the most peculiar of them all. The kitchen was her favorite hangout place. Learning from the royal chef how to cook, she wore commoners' clothes and was frequently mistaken for a maid. For audience at the royal court, she would arrive covered in flour, her clothes smudged with cheese sauce or beef stew, specks of dill or oregano in her hair. The king's advisors liked to play a game where they would guess what was for lunch by smelling Marushka. 'Sniff, Sniff,' they would take a few whiffs from a polite distance. 'Aaaaah! Roasted chicken for lunch today, yum, yum.'

"The king's advisors would tactfully suggest that Marushka was spending far too much time with commoners and was not developing royal mannerisms. The king told them not to worry: 'Some people are late bloomers; her royal blood will kick in at some point. I am certain of it!'

"The king's wife had died some years previously, leaving the king feeling bewildered with his parenting duties. One day, the eldest daughter consulted with her father. 'O father, should I wear the blue dress or the pink dress? Does the blue dress make me look fat?'

"The king stated the obvious: 'It is not the dress that makes you look fat; it's the fat on your ass that makes you look fat.' Oh, the hysterical production that followed! His daughter cried for days and wouldn't speak to him for two weeks after that. The poor king: 'Was it something I said? I only applied reason.'

"The second daughter came to him one morning complaining of strange cramps, and he instructed her, 'Go running around palace three times—cures all muscular ailments!'

"'You are trying to kill me!' she protested with a yelp. 'You don't love me, you don't understand me—you are ruining my life!' She walked away with a big huff.

"The poor king never knew what to do. Marushka would present him with a new concoction she'd made up in the kitchen, such as eggless egg salad, and the king would taste and spit it out. 'Yuck! Stick to the classics that the chef teaches—innovation is the enemy of the kitchen.' Marushka would wear a long face for weeks after that.

"The king had a secret that nobody knew. For most of the years he'd been king, he had consulted with his wife; she gave him the wisest advice and the most brilliant ideas. Then, with his wife's blessings, he would pretend that they were all his ideas.. Now that she was gone, whenever he was asked to resolve a problem or make an important decision, he didn't know what to say. He was the king, and he couldn't say, 'I don't know.' After all, if the king doesn't know, then who does know? If the king doesn't know, then anything could happen—pretty soon, there would be an Occupy Kingdom movement, and people would be marching in the streets and everything would turn into chaos.

"So instead of saying, 'I don't know,' he would delay. 'I know exactly what to do.' he would declare confidently. 'You are not ready to hear my brilliant proclamation yet; I will dispense with my wisdom when you are ready to receive it.'

"Everyone was impressed with the wisdom of the king— not only did he know all the right answers, he also knew when people were ready to hear them. Then, at night, when everybody was sleeping, the king would lock the door to his bedroom, light a tiny little candle and sit in a chair opposite a large oil portrait of his late wife. In that chair, he would think about what his brilliant wife might say. 'Dear wife, dear wife, please rescue me—what should I do?"

"Sooner or later, he would remember something his wife had said in the past in response to a similar situation, and he would get his answer. The next day, when he had all the right answers, he would again pretend that they were all his, same as before.

"His usual trick worked in all matters of state, but not with his daughters. All three would insist on an immediate reaction. They would stomp their feet and huff and puff. 'I want to hear what you have to say right now!' Each one felt that her dilemma was urgent.

"One day, after yet another hysterical debacle, the king felt despondent. 'I can't take this anymore. I don't know what to do, I don't know what to say, I am a horrible father, an incompetent king, I was a horrible husband. I quit! That's it! I will retire. I will move to Greece, buy a palace where nobody knows me, eat roasted meat every day, sit on a beach and forget all my troubles. But, before I retire, I must crown one of my daughters as queen. Which one should I choose?'

"The king scratched his head in confusion, and in the end, he decided that he would choose the queen based on which daughter loved him the most.

"He gathered all his officials, all his servants and all his daughters, and declared that he was ready to choose the queen. He asked his eldest daughter, 'Tell me, dear daughter, how much do you love me?'

"'I love you as much as all the gold in the world,' was her response.

"The king was pleased. 'You must love me dearly—all the gold in the world is very valuable.'

"Then, he asked his second daughter, 'You! How much do you love your king?'

"'O dear father, I love you, I love you—you are the wind beneath my wings. I love you as much as all the musical instruments in the world,' was her response.

"The king was pleased. All the musical instruments is a kingly present, indeed.

"Finally, he asked Marushka. 'Tell me, how much do you love me?'

"'Oh, I don't know,' she responded.

"'Come on! Try to quantify it,' said the king.

"'I suppose I love you the way a daughter loves her father.'

"'What? That is pedestrian!' The king was outraged. 'Every daughter loves her father; that is her duty. I am no ordinary father—I am the king! How much do you love your father, the king?'

"Marushka hesitated and tried to think of an answer.

"The king chimed in with a hint while pointing at the royal scepter, which was encrusted with rubies and diamonds. 'There are other valuable things besides gold,' he said.

"'I love you as much as I love salt,' she blurted out.

"The king thought he had heard wrong. 'What?'

"'I love you as much as I love salt,' she replied again; the answer was the same.

"'Salt is common—everybody has salt. It is cheap and nearly worthless. Change your answer!'

"'Father! Salt is more valuable than gold.'

"The king was so outraged, he kicked his daughter out of the royal palace.

"That night he tried to sleep, but he kept on tossing and turning in the royal bed. So he sat in the chair in front of his wife's portrait, but she was staring at him with a disapproving gaze and said nothing. 'Oh, great! The silent treatment. Exactly what I need right now.'

"On the one hand, he was worried about his daughter; but on the other hand, he felt justified in his actions.

"The next day, one of his advisors suggested that perhaps a search party should be dispatched to look for Marushka and bring her back. The king waved his hand and said, 'She will come back to apologize on her own.'

"Some crazy defiance overtook him. He felt compelled to prove that salt is not more valuable than gold. He ordered that all the salt from the whole kingdom should be gathered and destroyed. Then he ordered that nobody was allowed to use salt at all.

"Everybody from far and wide brought the salt they had to the palace, where it was collected in a large barrel. All the kingdom's salt was dumped in the river, and there was no more salt. The royal chef tried his best to compensate with herbs and spices, but no matter what ingenuity he employed, everything came out tasteless. Marushka's sisters complained that they didn't like their food. 'We simply need to adjust,' the king proclaimed.

"The next day, the chef was ordered to only make desserts. Cream puffs, chocolate cake, strawberry tarts—everybody was happy ... the first day. But by the end of the week, the sight of whipped cream and chocolate became nauseating to all. 'We want real food.' the two princesses wept.

"The king didn't know what to do. His wife—or shall I say, his wife's portrait—wasn't talking to him. The king couldn't possibly say that he was wrong, and he had nobody to give him advice. The princesses stopped eating, and their hunger led them to faint on occasion. Everybody in the whole kingdom started complaining, and some people began to emigrate.

"The king himself felt miserable, and was worried about his missing daughter. He stood at the window, staring at the stars. It was a starry, starry night. Suddenly the king became overwhelmed by a feeling of insignificance. Humbleness took him to a place where he had never visited before.

"The day that Marushka was kicked out of the royal palace, she walked and walked and walked, until she got lost in the forest, where she sat on a log and began to cry. There, she met an old lady with a kindly face who had magical powers which she only used for good. The old lady offered Marushka to come live with her in return for her help. So Marushka moved into the old lady's cottage in the forest, where she helped her with housework, collecting medicinal herbs and—her favorite task—cooking.

"One day, while stirring a fish soup, the old wise lady told Marushka that it was time that she returned home. Before Marushka left, the old lady gave her a salt cellar made of silver and told her to give it to her father.

"Marushka trusted the old lady, and did as she was told. When she arrived at the royal palace, everybody looked sad and tired. Marushka headed straight to her father's bedroom and presented him with the mighty gift. The king was so delighted to see his daughter, he forgot all his troubles in her embrace.

'Marushka, you were right—salt is more valuable than gold. Right now, I would give up all my mighty treasure for a pinch of salt. Most of the time, I don't know what I am doing; you are such a wise young woman. You shall be the queen.'

"'But Father, I am too young, and I still have so much to learn in the kitchen. I don't know how to make a soufflé, and those lemon merengue pies are a total mystery to me. I think you are the wisest king in these lands, because you are the only one who has the courage to say "I don't know." It would be a shame to leave your post while you are still in your prime.'

"The salt cellar that the old lady had given to Marushka was a magical one; it replenished itself after each use, thus ensuring that there was enough salt for all the kingdom's inhabitants.

"The king decided to stay on his post and move on with his life; he married a lovely widow with braided blonde hair and hips the size of a giant pumpkin. A huge banquet was held to celebrate, where all the food was salted twice.

"And that is how the king learned that salt is more valuable than gold. But there is something even more valuable than salt ... do you know what it is? Love. Love is the salt of life."

The next morning, I am awakened by Ralf. He finds me sleeping on the elevator's floor.

"Nelly! Nelly! Why are sleeping in the elevator? Why are you covered in dust? What were you doing here? Why is there a chair in the elevator?"

I am grateful that he wasn't pausing to hear any answers. He grabs my right elbow to steady me as I stand. Then he dusts my sweatshirt and sweatpants off by lightly smacking them with the back of his hand. We look in each other's eyes for a few seconds, and I can see how sad and pathetic I look in the mirror of his eyes.

He drags me by an elbow outside the building and into a nearby coffee shop, where he sits me into a chair. Then he brings me a cup of coffee in a paper cup and a muffin in a paper bag. I am at such a low, I don't mind the serving style and drink my coffee anyway in silence. I take a few bites from the muffin. The sugar and caffeine are soothing the anxiety flowing inside my veins.

"What is wrong? What is going on?" asks Ralf.

I say nothing and instead stare at my shoes.

"Did somebody break your heart? Or are you lonely?"

"Nothing like that; I just lost a friend."

"Look—emigration is hard. When I left the U.S. for one year, I thought I would go crazy. Adjusting to a new culture and all that can be really rough. I wasn't able to take it, and ended up coming back."

I can't tell Ralf about Elvi, Insekab or even Blair. So instead, I tell him the story of the Rocks in the Mayonnaise Jar. You can refresh your memory by rereading the second chapter, the one titled "Mayonnaise".

Ralf listens to me attentively with an open mouth. When I am finished, he looks bewildered.

"So what does that story mean? Are you saying that you are working too hard and your life is out of balance? Or are you saying that you have no friends to share a cup of coffee with? What does that story have to do with you sleeping in the elevator? You are such a mystery, Nelly. You speak in riddles. You say tons of things without ever revealing anything about yourself. I guess it makes you feel superior, like you are better than everybody. You are not fooling me. We are all a mess. Some of us are better at hiding it, that is all. I also know that emigration is not about what you came looking for; more frequently than not, it is about what we are running away from."

I sip my coffee and eat a few more bites out of my muffin in silence.

Finally, Ralf gets fed up staring at me. He drives me home with instructions to go to bed. "I will write an email to Jack and tell him you are taking a sick day because you are not feeling well. Get plenty of rest and see you at work Monday."

He waves at me as he drives away and I wave back, mouthing, "Thank you."

The Visit

I wake up as usual at 7:00 a.m. and have granola decorated with cranberries, pistachios and white chocolate flakes. I make an orchid design on top of my breakfast in honor of my latest victory. Although I have many things on my mind, I feel upbeat. The thought of resting for one day and allowing myself to explore my host city is lifting my spirits. I pack a sandwich, an apple and a water bottle, and head out the door. I walk in a leisurely pace, enjoying the sight of the cherry blossom trees. The sun shines with a satisfied gaze upon my face. A light hop invades my walk as if the spirit of a dancing fairy has taken hold of my body. A senseless optimism radiates from my stomach. I don't know how or why; yet, I believe that everything will work out for the best, just the same.

When I reach the National Mall, I feel overwhelmed by the size of the place, the vastness of all the buildings that are nestled along it. It didn't look so intimidating last night when I looked at the map. Clearly, a single visit to this place is not sufficient to explore it fully. Realizing that several future visits will be required, I let go of the idea of a systematic plan to visit all the buildings, and decide instead to let my whimsical legs lead me wherever they may. A systematic plan will be devised at a later point—let this day have no discipline whatsoever.

The first building I walk into is the National Art Gallery. Indeed, Ralf has spoken the truth—there is no admission fee required; only a security check at the door. A few people are required to open their bags for inspection; I squeak through without notice.

There are several levels inside, and each one is lined with grandiose halls containing artwork of various kinds. On the ground level are paintings by a supposedly famous artist called "Picasso." Most of them look like the whimsical drawings of an eight-year-old. Normally, at this point I would have been agitated at the thought of some curator wasting the public`s time with such unworthy artwork. But mysteriously, my good mood doesn`t allow me to feel agitation. Instead, I am delighted by the flighty playfulness of these paintings.

Luckily, the quality of the paintings improves once I have ascended to the next floor. Each wing contains paintings from a particular country and a particular era. Spain, France and Italy are represented with abundance. Surprisingly, there is no wing for Quari-ay-eh-ay. My favorite is the contemporary French wing, but there is something worthy to look at in most wings. Unfortunately, the beauty of the artwork is poorly contrasted with a ridiculously decorated rotunda. Imagine a statue of a young woman doing an arabesque on a pedestal surrounded by a circle of fake flowers of different colors that do not match, which in turn is surrounded by black columns. All this mess is sitting underneath a grandiose dome. Tourists of various nationalities are taking pictures and admiring it. Hey! I guess bad taste is not restricted to this city alone.

I walk out of the National Art Gallery feeling overwhelmed and tired. I don't realize that I have done so much walking, but I must have, since my feet are aching in my black leather shoes. I sit down on the white stairs of the gallery to rest my feet and replenish my energy. I eat my apple and drink some water. I feel energized after a short 15-minute break. Ready for the next adventure!

My feet then lead me next to the National Museum of American History. My adventure there is far less fruitful. First I see an exhibit of the dresses of America's first ladies. These are all just plain evening dresses that any woman could wear; there is nothing special about them other than the fact that a past first lady has worn it at some point. Any creation by Desdemona would have rivaled even the best gown on display here. I can't help but laugh at the idea of displaying plain dresses in a museum; even funnier is the fact the people are looking at them with admiration and pointing them out to their children as if they were seeing a treasure from an exotic land.

After that, I walk through a wing that is displaying objects from a distant war that must have happened in this land. I don't linger, as this holds even less interest to me than the dresses.

Finally, there is a section in the museum that shows the evolution of computers through different years. This part I do find interesting. From closet-sized machines to boxes that look like tables, I am amazed at how quickly this machine I use on a nearly daily basis has evolved. Probably Ralf used these old closet-sized machines when he was a university student. Luckily, I am spared all the anguish and have graduated directly into a fast and more elegant laptop that I can fit into my handbag. How lucky am I?

I leave the Museum of American History feeling tired; there is a strange ache in my left knee. I sit again on the outside stairs to give myself a rest. The sandwich gets eaten with appreciation. Suddenly the smell of the air around me changes. It smells the way earth smells right after it rains, only there is no rain. A heavy feeling situates itself around my hips, as if two hands are holding me there and pushing me into the earth. I come to the conclusion that I am feeling tired and ready to go home. Clearly, I will have to come back to investigate further at a later point, but for now, my body is telling me to go home and relax for the rest of the day.

I get up to walk home, but the ache in my left knee increases. How strange? I have never had any problems with that knee, nor my right knee, either. I limp away from the Museum of American History, hoping that moving around will make the pain go away. Instead, it only gets worse. I try walking differently—on my toes, on my heels—nothing helps.

I decide to take the Smithsonian Metro to the Foggy Bottom Metro instead of walking home. The pain just keeps on getting worse. I hope that I can find a coffee shop where I might sit down again, but no such luxury is available in the area.

After much hobbling around, my knee is now screaming with pain. "Stop applying pressure on me! Right Now!"

I stand on my right leg to give the left knee a break, and bend over to give it a massage. I don't think I can make it all the way to the Metro. I need to sit down somewhere. When I look up, I find myself in front of a building called the "Freer Gallery." I walk inside to find a comfortable chair to sit in. A pleasant security guard greets me at the door. "May I have a look inside your bag?" he inquires with a broad smile.

There is a "ting" sound resonating in my ears that emanates from his smile. His teeth are white and shiny, his skin dark and smooth. I have never been subjected to a search that I didn't mind until this day. I open my bag. He elegantly places a ruler inside to examine my belongings, and then thanks me and wishes me a pleasant visit at the gallery.

"Where do I buy a ticket?" I ask while looking in his dark eyes. That brilliant smile is flashed at me again, the "ting" is heard, and he explains that entry is free. For a second, it occurs to me to ask him to search my bag more thoroughly, since he has only had a brief look, but that strikes me as being goofy. I can't think of anything else to ask him, and so am forced to walk into the gallery and explore the art exhibits.

Then the most amazing thing happens. The pain in my left knee completely disappears, as if the radiant smile of the security guard has healing powers.

There are artwork and artifacts from the Orient. Oh what a delight it is to see an intricately decorated china plate from 4,000 years ago. That sense of history. Mesmerized by a wooden warrior statue from Japan, I forget about my knee and wander about the much smaller, yet more comforting gallery.

The place is empty. I swear I am the only visitor in the gallery. I imagine myself as a queen in a palace with all these treasures from all around the world belonging to me. And then I step into a room that is called "the Peacock Room." A pamphlet outside the room explains that this was a rich man's dining room, which was designed by an American artist named Whistler. It was meant to showcase his unique collection of china that he had purchased from the Orient.

Indeed, the room is dotted with shelves displaying china jars of various sizes. All the walls, ceiling, doors and even shelves are hand-painted with a peacock theme. I gasp, feeling overwhelmed by the beauty that surrounds me in every direction. In every nook and cranny, in every spot, there is beauty and harmony. A melody of green, blue and golden colors combine together to form a visual symphony that rivals everything I have seen before it.

I am stricken by a sense of humbleness that feels like an earthquake in my torso. From being a queen in her palace, I turn into an insignificant ant that is fortunate enough to behold such greatness. My hands shake. An urge to cry overcomes me. A few second later, my body trembles as if I am encountering a fever. An unpleasant energy is emanating from my tummy and shoots through my four limbs. It feels like a thousand little snakes are swimming in my veins, eager to find an orifice from which to exit.

Fortunately, the unpleasant feeling and trembling last for only 30 seconds. That is followed with a feeling of soaring, as if any minute, my feet might lose contact with the Earth and I am about to float up in the air, defying the laws of gravity.

Have I entered the shaky no-straight-line land that Ashley spoke of? I open my eyes more widely, attempting to absorb as much of the beauty as I can. No matter how long I look and how much I absorb, my amazement never ceases; my sense of feeling nourished by it never stops. A thought pops into my head: "If ever I manage to create a work of such perfection and glory, then I will consider myself to be a lucky person."

I walk out of the Freer Gallery still feeling like I am walking on clouds. Everything around me is the same, yet different. Everything is strange, but familiar. It feels as if I am looking, hearing, tasting and sensing for the first time. The cherry blossom trees look ever so beautiful. Each person I encounter seems like a holder of the secret of the universe. All the noise and bits of chatter carry within their folds the highs and lows of music.

I walk home in slow, deliberate strides and go straight to bed, where I proceed to cry in heaves. That night, I dream that I am swimming in an ocean and the waves are overcoming me. There is no sense of panic, no fear; I welcome each wave as it comes.

Seattle Again

The following Monday, I walk to work and arrive there around at 9:00. I press the button to the elevator, where four other people are waiting. My ride up is accompanied by four coffee-holding gentlemen. I amuse myself by the fact that all four are accidentally wearing black. I imagine myself being held hostage by four ninjas, or perhaps they are my bodyguards, protecting a VIP from the attacks of an evildoer. If only they would ditch the coffee tumblers, they would fit perfectly into my fantasy.

Finally, Ashley and Ralf finish bug fixing and we prepare to release the new software to Tenco. During our weekly meeting. Jack announces that he will himself travel to Seattle for the handover. He wants me to travel with him, since I made such a good impression on the executives of Tenco during my last visit.

This time I don't mind so much, since I am still in the creative phase of my new design and haven't yet started anything new. I am charged with training the Tenco staff on how to use the new software, and with giving a presentation.

I accept my assignment with a simple "yes." Only once I was back at my desk do I see the red stapler. I remember that my trip to Seattle will mean meeting Blair face-to-face again. A sense of panic comes. I try to remember that we had made up and have even exchanged gifts by mail. Meeting him face-to-face will not be awkward at all, I repeat to myself. I will act natural, and he will act natural, as well. Things will be fine! No more "Visual vs. Content " arguments will be had.

I look again at the pepper red stapler on my desk, and a sense of joy enters my heart. I'd better work hard on my presentation and training to eliminate any easy targets for criticism.

Ashley and Ralf go back to their regular chatter, which blends into the background like the hum of the traffic. It grow distant and muffled. Over time, I slip away into a distant land.

I make sure that I understand every single bit of functionality the Tenco application possesses. I go through every window, screen, dialog and possible work flow. I wrap my head around metal sheets and how they are manufactured, cut and shipped around the world.

After lunch, Ashley approaches my desk and begins by saying, "Did you know that I am part Native American? My father grew up in a residential school, where he was molested by a priest and—"

I interrupt him gently. "Dear, dearest Ashley, I am super busy preparing for my upcoming trip. Your stories are always long and heart-wrenching. When I listen attentively to what you have to say, I can't stop imagining the scenarios that you describe inside my head, and then later at night, I have nightmares. Then, when I don't listen to what you say and tune you out, I feel bad because I am not being genuine. Can you please keep your stories short and positive?"

Ashley pauses and looks into my eyes. It is as if we are seeing each other for the first time. I can see my own reflection in his eyes.

"In that case, I will leave you alone to your work, and come back when I can think of something that fits the criteria."

Ashley walks back to his desk. I hear him whispering something to Ralf. Ralf is whispering back, and both of them shrug their shoulders before they continue discussing in an audible voice some celebrity named "Brittany Spears," who is flashing her genitals in a public place where the paparazzi are taking pictures of her. I briefly overhear a tiny glimpse of their discussion before I tune it out and return to my work.

On Wednesday morning, I meet Jack at the airport. We check in together. Sitting in the lounge at the gate, Jack's mobile phone rings. He gets up to answer it away from me. When he comes back to his seat, he says, "That was just my wife, Shirley, updating me on the news on the home front."

"You were home half an hour ago—how much new news can there be?" I think to myself. "I hope everything is alright," I say instead.

"Yes, yes—things are great. My stepchildren were dropped off at school, and Shirley is planning to do laundry today."

I remember doing loads and loads of laundry on a nearly daily basis back when I was caring for my sick father. He used to sweat profusely; his bed sheets and clothes had to be washed every day. I feel thankful for the relief from this laundry duty. Now that I live on my own, I sometimes get away with doing my laundry once every two weeks, and sometimes even longer.

When we arrive at the Seattle airport, Jack's phone rings again while we are waiting for our luggage. Okay, we were waiting for *my* luggage, since Jack brought only a carry-on, and I had a substantially larger suitcase, which had to be checked in.

"Hello! Yes, hi, Shirley. Yes, I arrived at the Seattle airport. I am just waiting for the luggage." Then Jack walks away as if to keep me from hearing the rest of his conversation, but I am able to decipher a few phrases, anyway.

"Yes, of course she is here; we were on the same airplane. ... It makes sense that we take the same taxi; we are staying at the same hotel. ... Shirley! You are being ridiculous. She is not even my type! She has thunder thighs and is not even good-looking. ... "Okay, okay—I am sorry. Look! Just relax. I am here to work. ... Don't worry about the laundry; I will do it when I get home. ... I know you are capable of doing the laundry on your own."

Is he talking about me? "Thunder thighs and not even attractive." Well, I guess he has to say something to his wife so that she won't feel jealous. What a silly woman. If only she knew that the level of attraction between myself and Jack is at the sub-zero level. I wish I could call Shirley and tell her that Jack never addresses me except to issue commands. Her man is all hers!

Jack returns, stone-faced and impatient to get out of the airport. I remain silent, not mentioning what I have overheard. I wasn't anticipating this sort of complication on this trip. A sense of anxiety fills my heart, but then I think, "This has nothing to do with me. Jack's problems with his wife are his to deal with. I haven't done a single thing to cause this." I push the issue out of my mind, and focus on the presentation that I have to make.

That night, Jack and I are invited to dinner at an Italian restaurant. The CEO, CIO and operational manager are there to welcome us to Seattle. For some bizarre reason, I feel relieved that Blair isn't there.

"Darn! Stop worrying about it, Nelly!" I order myself. "Just act natural when you meet him tomorrow."

The restaurant is large. It looks like it could comfortably seat 200 people. All the walls are painted with murals from nature. A gazelle surrounded by trees, a man walking with a dog along a path, and a child seated on a swing in a park are a few examples. The decorations are overstated and lack harmony. After catching a glimpse, I ignore them so as not to soil my mood.

The place is half-full. There is lots of hustling and bustling, chattering and muttering going on. The waiters seem to know the CEO and the CIO, and they welcome us to our table warmly. One of the waiters even pulls out the chair for me, and then pushes it in to assist me in my seating procedure. What a lovely gesture.

The CIO declares in a loud, confident voice that he is Italian and is a frequent patron of the restaurant, and therefore, he will take the liberty to order for the whole table. I feel relieved, since the menu is full of words I have never heard before: fettuccine, mascarpone, al dente, scampi and many other Italian words.

After communicating with the waiter, the CIO proceeds to tell us stories about his adventures. From speed motorcycling to paragliding, this top executive is determined to risk his life in the most creative ways possible.

"Perhaps he secretly hates his job and is subconsciously attempting to end his life." This secret thought makes me wish I could laugh out loud. Then the CEO tells all about his new private airplane and how he learned to pilot it.

Unfortunately, I can't talk about my adventures outside of work. I remain silent, pretending to be the most boring person at the table. I nod my head and smile instead. I will have plenty of time to talk and impress tomorrow during my presentation.

At the restaurant, Jack's cell phone keeps on ringing. Each time, he excuses himself to answer it. He walks towards the washrooms to answer the phone, and then comes back a few minutes later. Jack gets up three times before the food arrives. Once dinner is served, I stop counting how many times he gets up to answer his phone.

Most of the dishes are pasta in different shapes, smothered in a variety of sauces. There is a large plate of grilled chicken, and another one with crab legs in wine sauce. The CIO tells us the name of each dish. Each one comes with a little story. There is the story of how his grandmother used to make lasagna from scratch. The right way to cut pasta with a golden blade. He describes the right method of chopping garlic. Then he tells us the symbolic meaning of each pasta shape. He points to one plate that is filled with a twisted tube-shaped pasta, explaining that it is called "strozzapreti," which means "priest strangling pasta."

"Imagine in a poor town in Italy—the only people who had anything to eat were the priests. At Sunday mass, people brought food to share afterwards. This pasta was designed so that a greedy person who attempted to eat fast would choke in the process. Hence the name."

I am now listening attentively to the CIO, without any need to fake my interest. This idea of making the food itself of a particular shape would no doubt be popular in Quari-ay-eh-ay. I can imagine myself sitting at a table in a far better decorated restaurant, telling a story about each dish laid out on the table. Star-shaped rice dishes, diamonds, circles, hexagons, etc. Each shape relates to a story from ancient Quari history. What a fanciful invention—I must suggest this to Uncle Miguel. He will come up with the best matches to each food shape.

The CEO interrupts the enchanted storytelling by declaring that he is hungry and wants to eat. Then he picks up one of the dishes and passes it around. I place two spoonfuls from the priest-strangling dish and place it on my plate. Everybody else helps himself, as well. We begin to eat. This is when the CIO starts telling me about the right way to enjoy pasta: "Pasta has to be cooked just right—not overcooked and not undercooked. This is the only restaurant that does it properly. If the noodle is overcooked, it is too mushy and disappears in your mouth. If it is undercooked, it is hard and gives you no pleasure on the tongue. The perfect pasta gives you long sustained pleasure that allows you to use every aspect of your mouth."

I am now paying attention to the taste and sensation of the food in my mouth. It is indeed a pleasure that goes beyond the visual element. What a discovery!

Next, I help myself to the crab legs, using my hands to crack the hard outer shell to get into the meat. My hands become sticky and smelly afterwards. I get up to wash my hands in the washroom so that I can continue enjoying the rest of the food. On my way into the washroom, I pass by Jack, who is standing outside with his ear glued to the telephone. I stand close to the inside of the door of the ladies' washroom and overhear what he is saying.

"Yes, of course she is here, but there is a bunch of us. It is not like we are having dinner alone. ... I don't know what she is wearing. She is wearing clothes. ... I don't know when I will be back in my hotel room—as soon as the dinner is over, I promise. ... Don't worry about the laundry, darling—just take good care of yourself."

I sigh in exasperation; poor Jack is being tortured. He is not even doing anything bad. I wish he had sent me here solo. I can easily do all the necessary work on my own, and he would have spared himself this personal torment.

The rest of my dinner is an enjoyable experience. We spend four hours at the restaurant when the CIO orders dessert, which is pastry puffs stuffed with whipped cream and covered with a chocolate sauce. Finally something that I am familiar with. Only in Quari-ay-eh-ay it would be decorated with chocolate shreds and sprinkles or confetti.

Jack receives yet another phone call, which at this point is ignored by everybody around the table. When he comes back, he looks alarmed. He announces that he needs to return home due to a family emergency. He asks to speak to me in private. We walk together to the proximity of the washroom area. "My wife, Shirley, collapsed in the supermarket 20 minutes ago. I am going to take a taxi to the airport right now to go and take care of my stepkids. I guess she felt overwhelmed taking care of the kids on her own, doing the laundry and grocery shopping and all that. I think she just forgot to eat—she always needs to be reminded to eat, and usually that is my job. Anyway! I am leaving you behind on your own. You know what to do. Right! You need to do the handover. I am certain that you will do well. You can call me on my cell phone if there are any problems. Actually, no! Please don't call me on my cell phone. Just send me emails. I will be checking in every few hours."

Nelair

I arrive at Tenco's headquarters at 8:45, where the receptionist leads me to a conference room to set up for my presentation. I sit at the end of the table closest to the projection screen and hook up my laptop to the projector. The first person to walk into the room is the CIO, who greets me with an enthusiastic handshake.

"Hello, hello, hello," he repeats as if he can't believe I am in front of him.

"Thank you for a most fantastic dinner last night and all the stories about pasta," I say, attempting to ingratiate myself to him hoping the presentation goes smoothly as a result. He sits to my right, not too far from my position.

The CEO and COO walk in while chattering about a baseball game they were planning to watch later in the day. Absentmindedly, they sit down at the head of the table. Suddenly they snap out of the bubble of their discussion and notice the other people in the room.

"Good morning, everybody! We're sorry—we were just talking about the game later today."

That is when Blair walks into the room, silently seating himself in the middle section of the table to my left.

"Act natural— we are not having an argument yet again in this presentation," my thoughts whisper so as not to expose my nervousness. I ask the CIO, "Should I begin?"

He nods "yes." "Everybody is here—we might as well!"

I raise my voice to grab everybody's attention. "Good morning. Thank you for coming to this presentation, where I will unveil the new software for Tenco's website. First I will go over the major features and work flows. Please feel free to interrupt at any point to ask questions. Does this sound good?" I grin with a fake smile; I can feel my cheeks hurting from the strain of it.

The presentation goes well. The CEO, CIO and COO seem pleased. All three ask many questions and are satisfied with my answers. Not one question stumps me; I feel proud of myself.

Blair sits sullen in his chair, not saying anything. I am not sure whether I should feel insulted by his coldness, or relieved by the absence of any snarky comments.

We end the meeting by agreeing that I will commence the training session the next day for Tenco's administrative staff.

There is nothing for me to do for the rest of the day, so I decide to go for a walk and explore the city of Seattle.

I have to say that Seattle makes Washington, D.C., look good by comparison. The buildings are drab boxes that make no attempt at pleasing the eye. Kind of reminds me of Ashley; he is a slob and he knows it, and he is perfectly comfortable and happy being a slob. Despite the dismal lack of aesthetic architecture, I feel buoyant from the success of the morning. A bounce creeps into my walk. After walking for a few blocks, I come across a marketplace by the sea. There are stalls selling all sorts of things. This is a great opportunity for exploration—all my work for the next day is prepared already, and there is no reason for me to sit in my hotel room with nothing to do. Perhaps I will shop for gifts for my friends back in Quari-ay-eh-ay.

At one stall, there is a large collection of CDs and DVDs. One CD in particular catches my eye. It has a picture of a naked baby swimming in water with a dollar bill dangling in front of him. Pictures of babies always make me swoon. The CD is labeled "Nevermind," by a band called "Nirvana." Although I have never heard their music, I am certain that this CD would make the perfect gift for Mr. Trevrel. Any musical group that is seeking Nirvana and is attached to the innocence of a baby is bound to make worthy music.

Next, I find a most adorable necklace for Desdemona. It has a computer embedded in it. On the outside it looks like an elegant silver necklace; but unknown to the naked eye, it has sensors which can measure the wearer's heart rate. This device would capture anything and everything that happens in front of the wearer; any time it detects a sudden jump in heart rate, it logs everything five minutes prior and continues rolling until you tell it to halt. It is supposed to capture all the best and worst moments of your life. I just know this is the perfect gift for

Desdemona, as she constantly complains about her failure to maintain a dairy.

For beautiful Juliette, I find a lipstick called "Antidote." It is supposed to be a lipstick with healing properties. If you ever feel unwell, you can simply lick your own lips to make yourself feel better. Juliette, with all her healing teas, will appreciate this novel concept.

I can't believe my luck at finding the right gifts for all three people on my list.

Next, I come across a book titled *How to Find Your Perfect Soul Mate*. I don't believe in soul mates. Nevertheless, I hope that it will inspire Ophelia to expand her search for a suitable husband. She has had her eyes set on the crown prince, but commoners who marry royals always have a difficult time. Plus, this particular crown prince is arrogant and slightly unstable mentally.

With this amazing lucky streak, I dare to hope that I might find a perfect gift for Uncle Miguel. What to buy for somebody with the most refined taste? In a dark and distant corner of the market, there is a stall selling nothing but socks. So many people have attempted to sock the sockless prince and yet failed. Is it possible that I might be able to grasp the nearly unattainable? I look at the rows and rows of socks in different colors. Their fabric contains different shapes and patterns. A few even have fringe or frilly ornaments hanging off the ankle. I have seen all of it in Uncle Miguel's sock drawer, and know in my core that these will not do. Then I notice some plain socks in a rainbow of colors. Usually, that is the sock section I ignore, but I remember the red stapler sitting on my desk back in Washington, D.C., and all the joy that the solid color has given me over the last couple of months. Perhaps something with a solid yet rich enchanting color will do the trick.

I start fingering a pair of green socks. In the desert, green is the most beautiful color. This pair is emerald green—the same green as in a peacock's feather. And that is when it hits me. The most brilliant idea my mind has ever conceived—a mismatched pair of socks. All the socks that Uncle Miguel has are matched sets, and that is why he isn't able to wear them. As the person who wrote the policy forbidding duplication in architecture, he has a natural aversion to anything that is an exact copy of something else. I will buy a green pair and a blue pair, and then send him a mismatched blue/green pair.

My euphoria at having found the perfect gift idea for Uncle Miguel makes me delirious with happiness. I have unlocked a great secret that has mystified all of Quari-ay-eh-ay, when the answer was simpler that a game of tic-tac-toe.

Clutching my shopping bags like I was lovingly holding the hand of a child, I look up and see Blair standing in front of me. We stare at each other, wordless, for five heavy seconds. Finally, I say, "Hello."

"Hello, Nelly—what are you doing here?" His question is tentative.

"I have the afternoon off, and so I decided to buy gifts for friends back in Quari-ay-eh-ay. What are you doing here?"

Blair wrinkles his nose. "I just came here to get some lunch." Then he relaxes his face and smiles. "Good job today on the presentation, by the way. I have to give it to you—the application looks good."

"Thank you! That means lots to me. I wasn't sure what you thought, since you were silent for the whole meeting."

"I have something on my mind; please excuse my silence."

"No biggie. I am glad you like what the application looks like. Wait until you get your hands on it and start using it—you will like it even more."

"I am about to have lunch at this diner. Would you like to join me?" Blair points his finger at a deli behind him.

"I would love to. I just finished shopping and am feeling hungry."

The diner is crowded, but we manage to find seating in one corner. I order a shrimp sandwich; Blair gets a club sandwich.

Awkward silence hangs in the air like a helium balloon the day after a birthday party. Should I mention our flame war? Or is it best to pretend that what happened online doesn't affect face-to-face reality? A strange sensation erupts in my stomach; a lava of heat is radiating in there.

"Thank you for the pen." Blair finally breaks the silence. "Ever since I got that pen, I have been more inclined to write by hand. I even wrote a letter on a physical piece of paper a week ago and sent it by snail mail. This is probably my first."

"I write letters on real paper all the time. Most of my friends back home don't use email."

"I realized that there is a unique pleasure in sitting down and taking the time to organize my thoughts to write a letter to somebody. The feeling of the pen between my fingers as my hand moved across the paper felt nearly meditative."

"I have never thought about it in those terms."

"Sitting at my desk and writing with ink makes me feel like one of those Victorian era aristocrats taking leisurely time to organize my thoughts into a missive while somebody else is breaking his back to keep me rich. It is not an unpleasant experience. I am grateful, though, that I don't have to wear a starched wig."

"Thank you for the stapler. Its rich solid color has inspired me to buy just the right gift for a dear friend with a highly evolved taste."

"You should try to use the stapler to staple paper. You might discover that you enjoy the sensation."

"I will give that a try."

I take the first bite from my sandwich. Mushy bits of shrimps smothered in mayonnaise ooze from the side of the sandwich down my chin. I place what remains of the sandwich back onto my plate and grab a paper towel to clean my face.

"Oh, no! I have been spending too much time with Ashley—I am beginning to act like him," I think. But the dreaded idea evaporates as soon as it appears. The heat in my stomach turns to icy cold from embarrassment.

Blair laughs. "That is why I never order the shrimp sandwich—it's a mess to eat!" He hands me his paper napkin so that I can clean up the rest of my face. I decide that it would be best to use a fork and knife to eat what remains of my meal, even though it's is technically the wrong way to eat this food item; I don't want to face further humiliation. I was having a perfect day until that point—why must something like this happen to ruin it?

The next morning, I am at the Tenco office, commencing a training session for eight Tenco employees—six women and two men. They all look eager to learn and ask many questions (or maybe they are just happy to get a break from their regular job!). Either way, I am happy to teach them, although I am mildly bored with what I am teaching. I wish I could tell them about my hit on Craigslist instead. Now, that would be an awesome thing to give a presentation about.

During the lunch break, I sit in Tenco's bright lunchroom. The walls are white and bare. People sit around round tables, chitchatting quietly. Blair sits down next to me and presents me with a plate of a mysterious-looking dip whose origins I don't recognize.

"Would you like to try this new dip that I made last night?"

"What is it?"

"I experimented with mixing roasted eggplant and roasted red peppers. I am surprised at how interesting it tastes."

"This reminds me of the baba ghanoush dishes I used to make in Quari-ay-eh-ay. I used to decorate it with scenes from the Sistine Chapel, to the delight of all my friends."

"I like baba ghanoush and almost everything made with eggplant, which is what inspired me to try making this new dish. Try it!" Blair urges me to try his new concoction.

"I don't know," I hesitate. "I am not used to eating anything that isn't decorated properly. Since emigrating here I have lowered my standards, but this isn't even garnished."

"Who cares about decoration or garnish? Taste it—aren't you at least curious?" Blair is becoming agitated at this point.

"I don't know; the color looks odd."

Blair becomes angry and raises his voice. "Not everything is about looks, you know; you should pay some attention to substance. For an intelligent woman, you have a superficial side that astounds me."

Blair storms out of the lunchroom in a huff, shaking his head as he walks out. I feel puzzled by his reaction. This man gets offended at all sorts of little stuff. Why does he care if I don't want to taste something? His behavior is a mystery to me. Maybe this is some special dish, or maybe he felt proud of his culinary creation and wanted me to give him validation. Or maybe this new recipe had some special significance to him. Roasted eggplant tastes just fine on its own, and so do roasted red peppers—why mix them? Why innovate on old classics? Plus, he called me "superficial." I am not superficial; I just care about good taste. I want to do things in their proper way. Is it wrong to wish to create harmony in the physical appearance of things? This physical harmony is meant to inspire harmony in people's hearts and minds. This isn't some shallow pursuit; this is a philosophy and a way of life! The world is full of diversity and conflict, friction and hostility. The Quari prime objective it is to find novel methods to combine diverse elements and place them side by side, creating a pleasing symphony without compromising on any note. This is the opposite of attempting to create a golden mean about which Aristotle spoke many years ago—which, in my view, only encourages mediocrity. I'd rather feel hot and cold in the same instant, to be both brave and cowardly, to embrace anger and compassion in the same action. Two extremes together, side by side. Contradictions, face-to-face without the predictable explosion. I do not seek the beauty you find in American fashion magazines or Hollywood movies, the kind that tantalizes your eyes and perhaps entertains for a few minutes. I want beauty that attacks your psyche and reprograms the way you look at the world, blows up your senses out of yourself. Anything less is trash.

Ok! You know what? I am sick and tired of tiptoeing around Blair. His moodiness, his temper tantrums and his criticisms of me. That's it! I will confront him, face to face.

I storm into his office and demand to taste his darned undecorated dip.

"I threw it in the garbage." His hands are resting on his desk, his fingers gripping with force as if he is afraid he might fall off the chair.

That is the end of our conversation. I have nothing to say, so I turn around and walk out of his office.

Irony

These days, I take the stairs at work. Perhaps Elvi needs some space. I had asked too much of him, laying all my problems at his brass doors, not once stopping to consider the heavy burdens he deals with. Ralf and Ashley assume that I am attempting to lose weight and get fit; they even tease me about it.

"Hey, Nelly! Will you be joining the gym soon?"

"I hear Pilates is all the rage these days with ladies who watch their figures."

My visit to the Peacock Room uplifted my spirit and gave me hope. I am certain that had I met James Whistler, the artist behind that miraculous work, we would have gotten along. That dining room contains everything I am attempting to achieve with my own work. Whistler was an American, after all, and this simple fact shines a faint light of hope that I will be able to reach into my audience. A country that is capable of producing a single man with such high taste gives me faith that good things are in store.

For fun, I call my next design "Operation Bust Irony" (OBI). For this design, I start by creating graphical sketches that will be the basis of the theme, instead of starting with the font which is then extended into all other elements of the design. I will design the graphics first and do the font last. Using my unique rocks-in-a-mayonnaise jar style, I draw a set of drawings depicting a bushy tree with a multitude of branches and leaves. The tree has equally abundant roots. At the top, I draw a human figure that seems to be growing out of the tree leaves, and at the bottom, a second human figure that is emerging from the roots. I draw a set that includes morning, night, afternoon and twilight. The human figures are appropriately drawn waking up, sleeping, facing away from each other and facing towards each other. My OBI theme will display a different set of graphics based on the time of the day of the person viewing it.

Once I have my hand-drawn sketches, I decorate them with my unique rocks-in-a-mayonnaise jar style. The final drawing are so hauntingly beautiful, I can't imagine anybody looking at them with one drop of cynicism. I arrive early to work so that I can scan the images before anybody is around to see what I am doing.

The font, I design with simple elegant lines, where each letter has either a tree branch with a single leaf sprouting on the top or a root emerging from the bottom.

After much thinking, I decide that I will install my newest design at Wikipedia.org. I will slice the image of the tree down the middle, where half the tree will appear on the left-hand side of the website behind the navigational elements. The human figures are to be situated one in the header of the website, and the second in the footer. I study the website by creating an account and making a few edits to some of the pages. Wikipedia is a website where anybody can edit the content. All of my edits are immediately revoked by Wikipedia administrators, with stern warnings about blocking my account. Woooh! These Wikipedians take themselves seriously. You would think they were in search of the secret of the universe or something.

After a few days of playful poking about, I am able to figure out a way to hack into the website. Finally, the day of installing my newest design arrives. I place all my hard work in place on the Wikipedia server, including the "hacked by Insekab" signature, and walk away from my computer to get a cup of coffee in the Snugoo kitchen. It is a place I usually avoid; it is usually a mess—dirty dishes in the sink, mismatched cups in the cupboards and stale food in the fridge.

My stomach is racing with nerves; I want to cry in anticipation of all the misunderstandings I am about to encounter with my newest creation. "O God! Give me the courage to get through this!" Will my irony antidote work?

I sit back at my desk with the cup of coffee warming my hands and place the mug against my chest, hoping it will soothe my heart, when I hear Ashley shouting out loud to Ralf: "Holy Cow!"

"What?"

"Insekab hacked into Wikipedia!"

"Shut up!"

"Go have a look!"

"Shut your pie hole!"

"I ain't kidding!"

"Ooooooooooooooooh!"

"Seeeeeeeeeeeee?"

"Yaaaaaaaaaaaaaaaaaa!"

"Yeeeeeeeeeeeoooooooooooo!"

"I know!"

"What the fuck!

"I know, I know!"

"Hmmmmmmmmmmm!"

"So different from the last one!"

"The dude had a style evolution!"

"I dig it!"

"I dig digging it!"

"Look at the bottom of the page!"

"I dig the roots!"

"The roots are digging the earth!"

"Makes me think of petrichor!"

The fact that Ashley and Ralf like the new design worries me.

"Hey, Nelly! What do you think of the new Wikipedia design?" shouts Ralf in my direction.

"Huh?"

"Go to Wikipedia and have a look around!"

"Okay."

"What do you think?"

"You mean that I should go check it right away?"

"Yes, go take a look right now!"

"Okay."

Three minutes later....

"I don't know." My voice is cracking with hesitation. "I guess I like it; it certainly is attempting to communicate something." I push out the words like chocolate Jell-O pressed through my teeth.

"Wow! Nelly, we actually agree on something—that is amazing!"

"It totally communicates to me, as well," chimes in Ashley, sounding delighted with our newfound group dynamic.

On Twitter, I read the following tweets:

#insekab outdoes himself

The man is a genius, how does #insekab do it?

Check out tree of knowledge design on Wikipedia

hacking is a form of vandalism, no different than graffiti #insekab

#insekab, marry me!

#insekab = #banksy?

The new #insekab links knowledge with human emotion, it says that Wikipedia is subjective

#insekab derides science in new design

We need to root knowledge with spirit, did I get that right? #insekab

#insekab is a graphical cyberterrorist

#insekab is a member of Al-Qaeda sent to corrupt western civilization with his wacky beautiful ideas.

I say he is a closet homosexual, something about #insekab's design is very gay

Two hours after the initial reaction, people notice that the graphics change with time. A new flurry of commentary floods the Internet.

This time I don't mind all the misconceptions so much, because I was anticipating it. At least some of the reactions are positive, which somehow make me feel some measure of fulfillment. The idea of a tree representing knowledge does appeal to me. I wish I could say that I had thought of it; however, how will anybody know that it wasn't my initial intention? I am surprised by how impressed people are with the fact that I managed to hack into Wikipedia, since it was actually relatively easy—it only took me four days to figure it out. If I can do it, almost any tech-savvy person could do it, too. That aspect of it is not at all impressive.

It still bothers me that I am assumed to be a man, and that people are reading all sorts of political and social messages into my design. But overall, I am satisfied I have made some inroads with my newest effort.

In the evening news, my latest hit is reported:

In other news today, Wikipedia, the free Internet encyclopedia, was hacked by a person or group of people calling themselves "Insekab." No personal information was accessed. An elaborate design was installed, inspired this time by a tree motif. Here is an interview with Jimmy Wales, the co-founder of Wikipedia:

"Since ten o'clock this morning, my email has been deluged with commentary on the new Insekab hit. About half the people hate the design and want it off the website right away. The other half love it and are demanding that we keep it. After a long discussion with the Wikipedia community, and in keeping with Wikipedia democratic traditions—where all is decided by a community of volunteers who do things for fun—we have come up with middle-of-the-road solution where we will keep it for three weeks, after which we will revert back to the old design. Wikipedia's lead software developer has analyzed the installed software, and he assures us that there are no viruses or malware installed in the hack. The tree design is totally benign; everybody using Wikipedia should feel safe to browse our website.

"Personally, I like the design; it looks much more sophisticated than that orchid theme that was installed on Craigslist. Probably Insekab likes us better than he likes Craigslist. Since the hack, visits to our website have increased threefold, and donations to our foundation have gone up by twenty percent. Although I don't support hacking, I have to say that this one did benefit us."

Recipe

Today I receive a letter—an actual letter written on a piece of paper—at the Snugoo office. This is a first at my workplace; all professional correspondence until now has been conducted via email. When I open the letter, I am further surprised that it is handwritten, not printed out. It is a letter from Blair.

Hello Nelly,

It seems that I am forever condemned to write apologies to you. I decided to write by hand using the pen that you gave me, hoping that I would be able to collect my thoughts enough so as to make this my last missive of regret to you. I am sorry about the way I behaved the last time you came to visit the Tenco office. I was not sensitive to your need to eat food that is served properly. Tupperware and no garnish is the norm in my world, but I guess it seems offensive in your culture.

I had invented this special recipe that combines eggplant and red pepper. After some experimentation in the kitchen, I came up with the right formula that results in superior taste. Perhaps you will do me the honor of finishing the recipe with instructions for serving and decoration. I am afraid that without your input, the recipe will forever be unfinished.

Recipe for Nelair:

It is absolutely necessary that you go out in person to purchase all the ingredients yourself. Walk in a leisurely pace towards the grocer, thinking well-intentioned thoughts. Caress each vegetable by hand and choose only the ones most agreeable to your senses. Here, I mean all of your senses—touch, smell and sight.

Ingredients:

One large eggplant or two small ones

Two red peppers

Four large, ripe tomatoes

Fresh dill

One onion

2 tablespoons of extra virgin olive oil

Dash of cumin

Salt and pepper

Cooking instructions:

Wash the eggplant, peppers and tomatoes and then pat them dry.

Please wear oven mitts while doing the next step, to avoid burning your hands.

Roast the red peppers under the broiler until dark splotches form all over.

Place the roasted red peppers in a plastic bag for 2-3 minutes. Peel and seed the red peppers. The plastic bag steam bath will make it easy to peel the red peppers naked down to their sweet essence.

Dice the red peppers into small pieces.

Pierce the eggplant with a knife at random places 6 times. Place in a baking dish and roast in an oven for 1 hour on 400.

Peel the eggplant, preserving the pulp, which should be mushy after the roasting.

Dice and fry the onion in the olive oil in a large frying pan.

Add eggplant, diced red pepper and diced tomatoes.

Stir occasionally, until the tomatoes are thoroughly cooked (about 30 minutes).

Add all the spices and mix.

You can serve this dish hot or warm, with a piece of bread or as an accompaniment to plain rice.

Can't wait to see what you will come up with,

Blair

Blair's letter has left me in a confused state. Is this some romantic gesture? Or is he my first convert in America? Is he on a mission to refine his aesthetic senses? Or is he attempting to get me to fall for him? How can I tell the difference?

My stomach starts grumbling as I contemplate the questions. My kidneys feel as if they are doing a Texas square dance, yet I have a stupid smile plastered on my face which no sooner do I place it under control, it creeps up again when I am not noticing.

After much contemplation, I decide that I have no choice but to finish the Nelair recipe, assuming the most positive intentions on Blair's part. I carefully fold Blair's letter and place it back in the envelope that it was sent in, concealing it in the pocket of my jacket.

I could do one of my usual designs inspired by the Sistine Chapel, but a creative recipe requires a creative new design. I will not be outdone. All those comparisons to Banksy made on the Internet have got me thinking that if I can get a couple of inspirations from Ralf, I can certainly allow myself to be inspired by a graffiti vandal. Stencils are a little utilized technique in food decoration, and it's about time I innovate in a little-explored space—to boldly venture where no aesthetician has ventured before!

I create a medium-sized stencil of a butterfly, large enough to fit two butterflies into the serving plate that I have. Then I go about experimenting. Carrying Blair's recipe in my pocket, I walk in a leisurely pace to the Whole Foods Market on Eye Street in my neighborhood, where I attentively select the ingredients. For my first attempt, I create fine cracker crumbs which I color in red and blue. Using my butterfly stencil, I create two imprints on the Nelair with the bread crumbs. This looks attractive, but it isn't impressive on its own.

There is too much food to be consumed by a single person, so I place my creation in the fridge and take it to work with me the next day. It is Wednesday, or "hump day," as Ashley likes to call it. I bring a simple tablecloth. I clean the kitchen, and wash all the dirty cups and dishes in the sink. I warm the Nelair in the microwave and place it nicely on the counter with small serving dishes and pita bread cut up into quarters. Then I send an email to Ralf, Ashley and Jack to let them know that I have brought food from home which they are welcome to. By the end of the day, the plate is wiped clean—there is nothing left except a few bread crumbs where the pita bread previously resided.

"I guess they really liked it!" I amuse myself with the thought.

The next Wednesday, I go through the same routine. I bring a tablecloth, clean the kitchen and serve the Nelair decorated with two butterflies. This time, the butterflies are created using grated cheddar cheese and finely-chopped tomatoes. It looks even worse than my initial effort, but I serve it to my undeserving coworkers, anyway. Five minutes after the invite email, I can hear Ashley, Ralf and Jack chatting in the kitchen.

Jack: "So what is the occasion? Why is Nelly doing this?"

Ashley: "Maybe it's her way of compensating us for putting up with her personality."

Ralf: "Come on, you do have to admit that this is delicious."

Ashley: "What's up with the butterflies?"

Jack: "You know Nelly—she just has to make everything pretty."

Ralf: "I am actually surprised that she has skill in the kitchen; she doesn't look like the type."

Jack: "What do you mean?"

Ralf: "Don't know! She looks like somebody who wouldn't condescend to cooking—the feminist type."

Ashley: "How come she never eats what she serves us? Do you think there something in the food?"

Jack: "Like what?"

Ashley: "Perhaps this eggplant dip is laced with estrogen that will rob us of our manhood over time."

(All three men break into laughter.)

Jack: "Oh, Ashley! I don't know how your brain works."

It feels odd hearing all three men conversing. It is a new type of dialogue that I have never heard them exchange before. In their voices, there is a softness. It isn't what they are saying, but rather the way they are saying it, that is different. Things never cease to amaze me at this place.

The next day, there is an email from Jack.

Subject: Team Building Potluck Lunch

Hello Team,

Inspired by Nelly's culinary skill, I have decided that we should all have a team potluck lunch next Wednesday. Please bring a dish from home, or if you don't know how to cook, then purchase something that you would like to share with your teammates. Let's meet at noon in the kitchen to share a bite to eat.

Regards,

Jack

Oh, great! I have inspired something that I didn't want. I only wish I could inspire the things I do care about. Since when does Jack care about team-building exercises? He hardly talks to anybody.

Ashley: "Whooooa! What does this mean?"

Ralf: "What?"

Ashley: "Read your email."

Ralf: "Ooooooo! This is new."

Ashley: "Nelly! This is all your fault!"

Me: "What did I do?"

Ashley: "You placed this cockeyed idea into his head."

Me: "Believe me! The thought of witnessing food that has been tortured at your hands is not something I would ever want to think about."

Ashley: "I happen to be a talented cook!"

I couldn't help but laugh at that.

Ashley: "No, really! I do know how to cook!"

Me: "I am sure that your definition of cooking seems valid inside your fantasy world."

Ashley: "You just wait and see."

Ralf: "Hey! I have an idea."

Me: "What?"

Ralf: "Let's have a competition for who makes the best dish at the potluck next week!"

Ashley: "What does the winner get?"

Ralf: "The winner will get $20 from each person who loses."

Me: "You guys are missing the point of the communal lunch. The idea is to build friendships and exchange goodwill!"

Ashley: "Said like a true woman—you are just afraid that you will lose the competition."

Me: "Fine—here is my $20."

Ralf: "Should we include Jack in the competition?"

Ashley: "Naaaah! We will be forced to lose to him—what is the fun in that?"

Ralf collected $20 from Ashley, added an equal amount from his own pocket, and placed the $60 into an empty box on which he wrote "Prize Money" with a black pen, and then he placed it in his desk drawer to be disbursed next week.

I am unsatisfied with my decoration efforts for the Nelair, and thus feel happy to try again next week. The only thing I am dreading is feeling obligated out of politeness to eat something that the stooges at my workplace have prepared.

My two decoration attempts so far have been disappointing, not a good enough match for the Blair challenge. I want something that looks as good as a decorated cake, yet with a savory taste to match the recipe. I need to come up with a savory icing recipe—icing without sugar; rain without wetness; beauty without a beholder; like somebody who wants to have sex but doesn't want to get dirty. All seem superficially possible, yet reality keeps them in remote islands where only skillful sailors have a chance.

My poor food processor goes into overdrive as I whip and mix different ingredients, hoping to achieve the impossible—an achievement much more difficult than hacking into the tightest website—to achieve the smooth, inviting texture of regular icing so that it can be piped into soothing waves, yet maintain the integrity of savory taste. I start by mixing butter and salt, but the result brings forth memories of atrocities of war from decades past. After several trips to Whole Foods Market in Foggy Bottom—where on the initial trip I had purchased the items scribed on a list in my notebook—on this, my fifth trip, I find myself throwing random ingredients into my basket, hoping against hope to stumble onto the impossible by an act of luck.

The hopeless sheds the "less" and becomes "more" at exactly 2:00 a.m. I will gladly share with you my miraculous discovery; please use it as frequently as possible to liberate the world of savory from the tyranny of sweetness.

I finally have everything I need to write a response to Blair.

Dear Blair;

Thank you for sharing with me the fruit of your creative imagination. I have made your recipe three times already, much to the delight of my coworkers who have twice already wiped my serving plate clean in their enjoyment of your special creation. I have attached a picture of the final product and a butterfly stencil that you will find handy. To your recipe, add an additional roasted pepper. While roasting the eggplant, add 5 unpeeled gloves of garlic to the baking sheet. Also 50 grams of Blue Chip tortillas which look mostly black. You will need the following:

Food processor

Disposable pastry bag or a heavy duty Ziploc bag.

Make the sugarless icing ahead of time by mixing all the below ingredients together.

Sugarless Icing:

1 can water chestnuts

50 grams cream cheese, softened

3/4 cup sour cream

1/2 cup mayonnaise

2 tablespoons grated Parmesan cheese

5 cloves roasted garlic

1/2 teaspoon salt

1/2 teaspoon lemon juice

1/2 teaspoon onion powder

Divide into two batches and add one red pepper to one of the batches to make red icing.

Crush the Blue Chip tortillas into fine crumbs by smashing them in a plastic bag. Using the butterfly stencil to create two butterflies facing away from each other by filling the area with tortilla crumbs.

Then pipe red icing into the wings of each butterfly wing. The black tortilla crumbs will create a nice backdrop, which will make the red icing pop. Finally, take the white icing and squeeze out little white drops lining the outline of the wings. Then place more white dots in random places on the dip, and garnish with finely-chopped parsley. This way, it will look like the two butterflies are flying through lush foliage.

Regards,

Nelly

At work, it is Wednesday . I make sure the kitchen looks suitable for our communal potluck lunch. I place a clean, white tablecloth, small serving plates and napkins, awaiting the lunch. When noon strikes, I rush to the kitchen to heat up the Nelair in the microwave so that it will be ready for my coworkers. Ashley follows me into the kitchen, producing a plate of fried rice that has shrimp, vegetables and little pieces of fried omelet. I am shocked that Ashley's dish actually looks edible. Although undecorated, it is attractive to look at because of the colorful contrast between the different vegetables and the rice.

"Did you make that yourself?" I ask him skeptically.

"Yes." His tone is defiant. "I learned to make it from my girlfriend when I lived in the Philippines. I knew that our relationship wouldn't last, so I made sure to learn how to make it before I left the country."

Ralf walks up from behind us, breathing down our necks as he inspects the dishes already laid out on the kitchen counter. "Not bad, not bad," he muses to himself, "but wait 'til you see what I brought." He dives into the fridge, thrusting his whole torso inside as if he needs to cool himself, and then emerges with a victorious smile. "This is Russian salad, the way my grandmother used to make it."

It is the first time I have ever seen Ralf with a smile of delight on his face. Then Ralf turns to me.

"Ever since you told me about the story of the rocks in the mayonnaise jar—which I still don't understand—I have been thinking about the Russian salad that my grandmother used to make. I haven't had it for years. When Jack told us about the lunch, I gave my mother a phone call and demanded the recipe. Turns out it is not that hard to make. You boil potatoes, carrots, peas and eggs. Grate some cheese and add mayonnaise to the whole thing."

Ashley quickly chimes in, "What is the story of the rocks in a mayonnaise jar?"

Ralf: "Oh, I don't know—some weird story that Nelly told me."

Ashley: "I didn't know that Nelly told stories—how come you never told me a story?"

Ashley looks at me with the intensity of a burning lump of coal. I know I should look away, but I am not able to.

Me: "I don't have a story to tell you."

Ashley: "Then tell me the story of the mayonnaise and rocks."

Me: "It's a stupid story. Like Ralf said, it means nothing."

Ashley: "I want to hear it, anyway."

Me: "Errrrrr!"

Ashley: "Is it about a fool who puts mayonnaise on rocks to make them tasty?"

Me: "No."

Ashley: "Is it about making mayonnaise out of rocks and mud?"

Me: "No."

Ashley: "Is it about a bunch of rocks that want to find mayonnaise as icing for their mud cake?"

Jack walks into the kitchen, rescuing me from having to say "no" twenty more times. Silence pervades the kitchen while he, our fearful leader, smiles at all the food laid out in front of him. "Wow! You guys outdid yourselves!" Then he adds his contribution to the offering: a platter with three different types of cheeses and crackers. Jack never ceases to disappoint me. I do, however, have to confess that I feel pleasantly surprised at both Ashley and Ralf; both have made an effort, and both have produced something that looks edible. Ralf's Russian salad is even garnished with chopped parsley and caviar.

The time for admiration is over; the time for the four of us to partake arrives. We each take turns sampling from each plate.

Jack: "This is such a good idea, I think we should do this once a month."

Ashley: "Aha!"

Ralf: "'Hmmmmm!"

Ashley: "Nelly! How come you keep making the same thing—don't you know how to cook anything else?"

Me: "Oh! I was unhappy with the way I decorated the other two attempts. Now that I have created the perfect decoration, I can feel free to move on to other dishes."

Jack: "Do the butterflies symbolize rejuvenation in the work place?"

Ralf: "Everybody knows that a butterfly means flightiness or flakiness."

Ashley: "You both have it wrong—two butterflies always symbolize romantic love."

All three men look at me in an effort to surmise the slightest gesture that would betray my true meaning. I enjoy this air of mystery that surrounds me for a few minutes.

Me: "It doesn't mean any of these things; I was attempting to capture a sense of harmony in diverse elements, like the diverse ingredients of the recipe. Two butterflies flying away from each other, yet connected by a common destiny. They have shared a brief moment together, like we are sharing this lunch."

Jack: "Yes, like in teamwork. We all work towards the same goal, yet each one of us contributes differently."

We spent the rest of the lunch talking about teamwork in the office. I sample a little food from each dish. Each offering tastes good—even the cheese that Jack brought is delightful. My biggest surprise happens when I taste the Nelair, which is the very last thing I ate during this meal. A dance of flavors erupts in my mouth. Nelair tastes creamy, despite the lack of dairy in the recipe. I feel the urge to swipe my finger across my plate and lick every morsel of food off my own flesh. It is only a sense of propriety that prevents me from following my impulse. Tasting something so fantastic is making me feel uncomfortable, as if I need to go to the washroom yet am unable to. Food such as this is probably dangerous in ways that I can't explain. It assaults my taste buds with an alluring magnetism, like a mermaid singing her way into the heart of a sailor right before she is about to drown him.

"Nelly's dish is still the best," Jack declares in a commanding voice right before he exits the kitchen, concluding our lunch hour.

Ralf runs to his desk and comes back to present me with the prize money from his desk drawer. "Here, Nelly—Jack settled the competition—you made the best dish."

I suddenly feel uneasy with winning the competition. Although I agree that my dish is the best-tasting and by far the best-decorated, I wish I could express to Ashley and Ralf how much I appreciate the effort they made with their dishes. I feel happy and sad—both at the same time and in equal measure. I hesitate for thirty seconds, and finally say a polite, "Thank you."

Manifesto

Nobody understands what I am trying to accomplish. Unfortunately, I can't explain it to all the dummies who are interpreting my work wrongly, but I can explain it to you. I had thought it was obvious and didn't bother to, earlier. Now I am starting to suspect that you don't get it, either, but perhaps you feel too awkward to ask and expose your ignorance. No worries—Nelly is here, at your rescue.

My work is not art, although elements of it might be described as artistic. Art is trash in my view. An artist is somebody who labors for years and decades constructing some beautiful, imaginary fantasy that he feels compelled to drown himself in before he emerges half-dead on the shores of sanity to share with lemmings what a glorious discovery he has made. The assumption of such a tedious pursuit is odious to me; it divides humanity into a talented few and the untalented masses. No wonder multitudes of so-called artists commit suicide, go crazy, overdose on drugs and end up chopping off their ears. I would want to slash my wrists as well if I tried to become an artist.

In Quari-ay-eh-ay, there are no artists and no art galleries, and we don't discuss art. Everybody is an artist, and every surface reachable by human hands is an art gallery. From the clothes we wear to the walls of the buildings in which we dwell, all is fair game for everyone to allow their imagination to go wild. Our goal is not beauty, although it is easy to be misconstrued as such; our goal is to achieve harmony within the diversity. It is a communal activity in which everyone is expected to participate—nobody is excluded, no matter your intelligence or station in life. No individual is attempting to express himself; even a monkey is able to express itself—there is nothing exceptional about that idiosyncratic pursuit. Each is entering into a communal dialog, wherein the aim is to find a constructive improvement over what already is. It keeps our hearts pure and our thoughts aimed towards fruitful activities. It is oh, so easy for a human being to indulge in criticism and sink into a well of egocentric sense of self-righteousness. It is harder yet to dwell in such dark caves when your community is surrounding you with the warmth of continual inspiration.

Quari-ay-eh-ay is a country formed by many waves of immigrations from desperate corners of the Earth. The citizens of my dear motherland are followers of different religions, schools of thought and persuasions. We could have chosen to enter into debates which would result in endless arguments that might culminate in hurt feelings, anger and, who knows, maybe even violent acts. For generations now, we had found a unique method to create harmony while respecting our diversity, and this method has served us well.

Making a social, political or artistic statement is the furthest thing from my mind with my work. My only wish is to inspire each and every person in the world to participate in creating the virtual world which might become a transitional step to creating the physical world at a later point. Take ownership of the world you inhabit. A website that you visit belongs to you as much as it belongs to the people who built it. The same goes for the corner store where you purchase your groceries. By leaving a constructive mark, you gift others the treasure of your presence and therefore make yourself receptive to what they have to contribute. These creations are alive, for they are constantly changing, being embellished with layers of contributions. Nobody takes credit. The sentiments of the community are reflected for all to see. If one part is ailing, the rest will respond with healing vibrations. Nobody gets left behind. We all move forward, standing side by side, holding hands.

Placing a brilliant work of art in a decrepit building where it is gazed upon with admiration by the multitudes serves no function other than to aggrandize the cult of the artist. A false prophet who leads the flock towards further enslavement. My path is that of mass liberation. Admire nobody, and leave your own mark.

Fish

Thinking about my bitter breakup with Elvi, I wonder whether we will ever speak again, or if we will one day find our way back to a friendship. It reminds me of the story of the fish. This story was told to me by my mother when she was in the hospital, which was told to her by her mother. It's possible that the story has been distorted through the act of passing down of narrative tidbits. It's a good story, and I will attempt to tell it to you in the same fashion that I heard it. To tell you the truth, I was a bit aghast when my mother told me this tale; I was 13 years old at the time, and found the whimsical details strange. My mother was a prim and proper lady. At the time, I attributed the break with her character to the powerful sedatives she was prescribed. Perhaps all those nights reading Dr. Seuss to me when I was little had affected her. As I matured, I grew to like the story and see a deeper meaning in it.

Sometimes, things go wrong. In every life, there are times when things go wrong. Perhaps you break a nail. You just spent a fortune getting the best manicure you ever had, and your nail breaks. Or perhaps you wreck your car. Or perhaps somebody breaks your heart. So what are you going to do? I will tell you what you will do when things go wrong. You have no choice but to roll up your sleeves and keep moving on. It really is that simple. Which reminds me of the story of the fish.

There once was a fish that swam happily in the sea and was as happy as ... well, as happy as a fish swimming in the sea could be. One day, when the happy fish was swimming near the shore, it heard a wise voice from above say, "A woman needs a husband like a fish needs a bicycle."

The fish felt riveted by what it had heard. "A bicycle! A bicycle! A bicycle!" The fish repeated the word in its mind like a chant. "Oh, something that I don't need," thought the happy fish lustfully. "For once, to have something that I don't need—that would be something, indeed!"

And so the fish swam around the sea, feeling slightly less happy than happy can be, singing to herself a tune that can never be: "I want to ride a bicycle, I want to ride a bicycle, I want to ride a bicycle."

And then one day, as if by magic, the less happy than happy can be fish took a wrong turn and felt lost in the big sea. In a panic, the fish twirled around and zigzagged in random patterns until it found itself in a never before encountered reef. As the sun sent its golden rays down into the shallow end, darkness receded the way theatre drapes part on an opening night, and there it was—a shining object with two wheels. The fish's heart skipped two beats and wobbly wobbles went up and down its imaginary knees. "God is indeed great," professed the fish. For it had wished, yearned and asked, but only an empowered creator could have answered back so eloquently. The fish stared at the bicycle in awe, and with great trepidation, approached it attentively. First the fish had to untangle the weed that had entwined itself around the frame and across the wire. Then the fish made sure to place a colored ring around the wire of the front wheel to mark it as taken. The fish was certain that had any other fish discovered this treasure, it would lay its immediate claim.

Now that the bicycle was cleaned and marked, it still looked unsatisfied. The fish knew that a bicycle was made for riding and not lying on its side. That is when the fish realized that her imaginary knees and knuckles had better materialize. And so the fish swam to the Odd Objects store, where little fishes go to play pranks on their cousins and buy Halloween trappings. Along the soggy shelves it found mainly sandblasting guns and plastic fins, but at the back of the store, in the "Dropped From Heaven" department, it found what it desired: prosthetic human limbs, with the necessary knuckles and knees. The fish purchased without even asking the price, and went home feeling much accomplishment. The fish spent all of the evening strapping on legs and arms, and practicing wobbling motions to bring them alive. After many failed attempts, the fish felt confident. It decided to approach the prized possession in her new disposition. The bicycle seemed mildly impressed with the fish's hearty attempt, but, alas, all riding trials ended with the fish buried under a pile of arms, legs and bicycle.

The fish was now the most unhappy fish in the sea. It practiced and practiced with wobbly motions of all kind until a precise choreography of torso movements yielded mastery of the limbs. The unhappy fish thus approached the bicycle with a new determination. And lo and behold! A riding experience was in the cards. The fish rode gingerly, around and around in a circle, and then in a straight line. All the creatures of the sea looked upon the fish with amazement. Even the octopus and the shark spared precious moments to notice. The tortoise smiled for the first time in fifty years, and the starfish took a vow of non-violence. For times, they are changing—and the signs were clear as can be. They sensed that they had witnessed history.

The fish puffed up its chest in victory and rode around every day to much applause and adoration. The bicycle seemed pleased, but not all was well in the sea. A few logical fishes doubted the victorious fish and asked annoying logical questions: "Why ride a bicycle when you can swim faster? Why defy nature when God gave us scales and fins? A fish is not a human. Pretending to be something that you aren't is a dangerous venture." But the victorious fish answered them all with clever retorts that silenced them: "You dumb doubters—don't you see? This is progress; it is called technology. Today I ride gingerly in a straight line; tomorrow, I will zip around like a devil on ecstasy. You old-fashioned fish don't matter; it is us modern fish who hold the future in our nonexistent fingers."

In this state of defiance, the fish knew that she had to perform. In order to ride with the required speed, the defiant fish needed to construct an elaborate plan to level paths and roads so that the bicycle could speedily navigate around. Although the doubters had been silenced, the defiant fish was certain that their doubting voices would rise again.

As the vigorous training program for bicycle racing began, the astonishing happened: the bicycle spoke. Its first words in the sea were the screeching, moaning sounds of whining: "Eeeemmmmmmmmmmm ... I do not like to forge ahead with this haste; I do not enjoy being ridden by a fish; I do feel nauseated by the wetness of the salty sea."

The shocked fish was dumbfounded. Completely aghast, she inquired, "Why didn't you say something sooner? Until now, I thought you were deaf and mute!"

"Oooooooooh! I was lying there abandoned for a year when you found me. I didn't want to seem excessively fussy," replied the bicycle.

"That bastard! ... er ... I mean ... That illegitimate love child of a car and a unicycle! ... After everything I have done for him!... er ... I mean, After everything I have done for it!" The shocked fish began to scream, and in complete hysterics, picked up the bike with all her might and threw it to the shore. As tears poured down the depressed fish's cheeks, she took off the fake limbs. Much to her surprise, she found that real limbs had began to grow out of her torso, and the depressed fish realized that she had forgotten how to swim.

The fish sat next to the shore and sobbed and sobbed and sobbed. "O! One day, when I am finished sobbing, I will teach myself how to swim using these new limbs; who knows—perhaps I will invent a novel way of swimming for fish," said the depressed fish to console herself. "And if that doesn't work, I have heard that they can do wonders with plastic surgery these days," the depressed fish continued.

That is when the depressed fish again heard the wise voice from above: "I told you that a woman needs a husband like a fish needs a bicycle. Next time, why don't you poke yourself in the eye, instead, and save yourself the heartache!" And so the fish started a poke-in-the-eye business, where the young and foolish fish could, for a fee, get a poke in the eye—using the depressed fish's new limbs—to immunize themselves against heartache. Her business motto was, "A fish needs a bicycle like a woman needs a husband." And the fish lived bitterly forever after.

Food Processor

Today I received a handwritten letter from Blair.

Dear Nelly,

I got your instructions for the Nelair decoration. First thing I had to do was purchase a food processor, which I did right away. I had to make Nelair several times before I was able to perfect the butterfly shape using the stencil you so kindly provided. I think that I've finally mastered your technique, as evident by the picture attached of my latest attempt. I will let you judge for yourself. My roommates have been ruthlessly making fun of me because of my constant experimentation in the kitchen. It was when I purchased the food processor that the shit hit the fan. The next day I got a phone call from my mother, who was worried that there was something wrong with me. I assured her that everything was fine. The fact that I had sent her a handwritten letter few weeks previously didn't help to alleviate her concern. Rajeev thinks that I am developing an interest in cooking and that I am about to throw away my career as a computer programmer. Jim thinks the food processor is my coping mechanism as a result of stress at work. Ryan is beginning to suspect that I am a closet homosexual, as evidenced by the butterflies I have been decorating the food with. My mother is worried that I've joined a strange cult that spurns modern technology; why else would I send her a handwritten letter, when email is so accessible? All of this concern has made me laugh. Some people just don't understand how to enjoy the simple pleasures in life. I finally managed to calm everybody down. All three of my roommate love the Nelair. Each time I've made it, they have licked the plate clean. Rajeev especially loves the mixture of flavors, although he thinks I should make it spicier. I ordered them to enjoy the food and leave the psychoanalysis for when I am in an actual crisis. Have you managed to taste the Nelair? If yes, please let me know what you think of the taste.

All the best,

Blair

At work, Ashley continues to pressure me to tell him the story of the rocks in a mayonnaise jar.

Ashley: "Nelllllllly! When will you tell me the story about the rocks and mayonnaise?"

Me: "Never!"

Ashley: "How come you told Ralf the story?"

Me: "It was a lapse in judgment."

Ashley: "Ralf! Tell me the story that Nelly told you."

Ralf: "I don't remember all the details. To tell you the truth, I didn't understand it!"

Ashley: "Tell me the major highlights."

Ralf: "Okay! Some professor, I think, gets a clean mayonnaise jar. And shows his students how you can put rocks, pebbles and sand inside."

Ashley: "What for?"

Ralf: "I guess to teach them a lesson of some sort."

Ashley: "What was the lesson he was trying to teach them?"

Ralf: "I forget. I think it had something to do with fitting everything in neatly."

Ashley: "You mean like cram everything, like when we work overtime, go crazy and try to do several months' worth of work in a couple of weeks?"

Ralf: "Yeah! I guess that was the point."

Ashley: "Why the mayonnaise jar? Why not any other jar?"

Ralf: "I guess because mayonnaise is full of fat and calories and that symbolizes all the junk food that hard-working people like us must eat."

Ashley: "Ooooh, I'm beginning to like the story. What happens next?"

Ralf: "One of the students pours coffee into the whole mess."

Ashley: "Why?"

Ralf: "Caffeine and calories ... major coping mechanism of every geek."

Ashley: "Then what happens?"

Ralf: "Nothing—that is the end of the story."

Ashley: "This story is missing something."

Ralf: "Like what?"

Ashley: "Nicotine!"

Ralf: "Yes! Brilliant! Perhaps the mayonnaise jar filled with rocks is really a giant ashtray for smokers."

Ashley: "Yes, yes—that is a brilliant story—a story that makes you want to think."

Ralf: "A story that has real meaning."

Ashley: "There is one more thing that is missing from the story."

Ralf: "What is that?"

Ashley: "It's the most important element in any good story."

Ralf: "What!?"

Ashley: "Sex."

Ralf: "Yes—sex!"

Ashley: "Any story without sex is worthless."

Ralf: "Garbage!"

Ashley: "Perhaps this creative ashtray is to be used for a smoke right after sex, the way they used to do it in black and white movies."

Ralf: "Brilliant! An after-sex ashtray."

Ashley: "We should patent that idea!"

Ralf: "We should sell it on the Internet!"

Ashley: "We will become bazillionaires!"

Ralf: "Too bad smoking is out of fashion."

Ashley: "Our invention will make it fashionable again!"

Ralf: "Nelly's invention."

Ashley: "Yes, let us call it 'Nelly's after-sex ashtray'."

From that day on, Ralf brings to work mayonnaise-based food (chicken salad, tuna salad, macaroni salad and Russian salad). Ashley uses the empty mayonnaise jars to build prototypes for the after-sex ashtray. He uses colored sand and rocks, and each one is more beautiful and more elaborate than the previous one. I am both horrified and mesmerized by what I have inspired.

Kidney

I will spare you the discourse on the symptoms of the illness that befalls me. Suffice it to say that for the first two days, I believe I have the stomach flu. On the third day, I finally realize that there is something horribly wrong, and I go to see a doctor. I am diagnosed with a kidney infection and prescribed strong antibiotics, which make me feel worse. The doctor promises that the medication will make me better eventually. There is just one symptom that I will share with you, because it is spectacular. I am suddenly seized with the feeling a being hot and cold at the same time. Not hot and then cold. Not something in between hotness or coldness. Rather, hot and cold in the same instant, and in every molecule of my body. I sweat profusely in a feverish daze, and at the same time shiver violently as if the snow of the artic has enveloped me in my ailing state. My teeth chattering make such a loud noise, it nearly sounds comedic. This paradoxical state seizes my body four to five times a day, and I lay helpless, unable to combat it. What am I supposed to do when I am both hot and cold? I can't put on an extra sweater, nor cover up with a warm blanket. I can't use cold compresses. I can't crank up the heating in my apartment. There is nothing to do but to endure the experience of it.

To tell you the truth, there is something enjoyable about these episodes. They are dramatic. They are passionate. They encompass every fiber of my being. The surrender to it feels terrifying yet delicious. I feel as if my body is invaded by an alien force. At times, I feel that it might demolish my insides; at other times, I hope it will eat away all the rubbish of my life and leave only what is pure and good.

In the end, I spend a total of three weeks away from work on sick leave. Most of the time, I lay on the couch of my living room, staring out of the window at the sky, with only short excursions to the nearby Whole Foods supermarket to replenish my food supplies. Jack is understanding about my absence from work. He told me to take as much time as I need to recover. I called him on the fourth day of my illness and told him that the doctor has advised total bed rest for two to three weeks.

"Take as much time as you need—luckily, things are slow at work right now," was his reply. In truth, I am not missing going to work five times a week. It feels like a relief to do nothing all day long. I am so sick that I am not able to even focus on reading a book or enjoy watching a movie. Total rest was in the cards for me—Rest from thinking, feeling, planning, dreaming, imagining, worrying, talking and saving the world. Silence and rest are my daily routine. Toast and jam are my daily meal.

Luckily, I receive letters from Quari-ay-eh-ay, which provide for some comfort. I read each one in a drugged-up haze, attempting to string words into sentences that the fog of my mind is blocking.

Dear Nelly,

Thank you for your beautiful gift of the "Nevermind" CD by Nirvana. I have listened to it about one hundred times already. I look forward to many more listening experiences for further contemplation. It has a hypnotic effect on me which I can't explain. Have you listened to the song, "Smells Like Teen Spirit"? It is the best song I have ever heard in my whole, entire life. Those lyrics are expressing devotional love towards the divine. My favorite verse is when the singer seems to be repeating "Hello, Hello, Hello." I believe he is actually saying "Halo, Halo, Halo"—a search for saintly inspiration. I have been repeating it to myself like a mantra for weeks. Finally, it hit me: I need to draw images of saints with halos and give them away for free to comfort people. In place of giving away bookmarks, I have started hand-drawing haloed beings. I don't need to tell you who I started with; it was dear Mother Teresa. Although she hasn't been canonized yet, nobody deserves sainthood more than she, in my eyes. I make sure to include her image for anybody who seems lonely or isolated, hoping that it reminds them that somebody accepted all, even those rejected by everyone else. I have embarked on an extensive study of saints. Did you know that nearly all religions in the world have the concept of a saint? There are thousands and thousands of them—perhaps tens of thousands, perhaps more. There is so much work to do, and I am afraid that there aren't enough years left in my life to cover it all. I have included an image of my newest discovery—Saint Rabi'a al-Adawiyya, whose depiction I have included with this letter as a small token of gratitude for the gift you have sent me. Rabi'a was so devoted to God that her master felt compelled to free her from slavery, after which she led a life of such exemplary behavior, people travelled from far and wide to catch a glimpse of her light. I hope that you find comfort in contemplating this image, and may you be a beacon of light that shines on all near you.

With love;

Mr. Trevrel

Had I known that the CD was of religious devotional songs, I wouldn't have bought it. My goal was to buy something fun and playful for Mr. Trevrel. I seem to be cursed to be constantly inspiring people in the opposite direction than the one in which I intend. Oh, well! I guess drawing pictures of haloed saints isn't as bad as some of the other dreadful things that I have inspired thus far.

Dear Nelly,

Thank you for the mismatched pair of socks. Sometimes you don't know what you are looking for until you see it in front of your eyes. I never knew why I felt an aversion to socks until your package arrived in the mail. A big Aha! moment dawned on me. I have been wearing your delightful gift on a daily basis, much to the amazement of Quari-ay-eh-ay. My new sockful state is the talk of the whole town. Everybody wants to know who socked the sockless jewel of Quari-ay-eh-ay, and I am making certain to mention your name in every conversation, especially within earshot of a royal presence. I am hoping that this will help pave the way to your future employment in the royal palace when you return home. Your uncle always has your best interests in mind.

There has been an unfortunate development at the royal palace recently. The king has fallen ill, complaining of an acute pain in his left ear. We are all praying for his speedy recovery. The crown prince seems particularly seized by melancholy over the king's health. Some of his behavior is erratic. I once caught him talking to himself while walking in a hallway in the royal palace. His words were poignant and eloquent. I am doing my best to comfort him in his distress and assure him that his father is a strong and heroic man. A little earache will not be the end of him. I hope that I find the right words and the suitable course of action to keep our beloved royal family in a state of equanimity.

With gratitude,

Uncle Miguel

Instead of feeling happy, I feel sad at the realization that purchasing the right pair of socks for Uncle Miguel has been my only accomplishment this year. What if this is my only accomplishment in my entire life? That would be a rather pathetic life. Things had better turn around soon—otherwise, I am in danger of being the teller of the unfulfilled potential of the greatest story on Earth. I just need to regain my physical strength. I am certain that I can turn this around. You just wait and see.

On my fifteenth day of illness, I got a phone call from Ralf.

Ralf: "Hello, Nelly—how are you?"

Me: "Who is this?"

Ralf: "It's me, Ralf, from work."

Me: "Oh, hi, Ralf."

Ralf: "How are you feeling?"

Me: "Like a 90-year-old woman—I lay on the couch all day and get exhausted when I make the trip from living room to the kitchen."

Ralf: "Did you hear what happened at work?"

Me: "No—what happened?"

Ralf: "The elevator blew up."

Me: "What? What do you mean, 'blew up'?"

Ralf: "The engine somehow caught fire and exploded. Luckily, the sturdy elevator shaft contained the impact of the explosion. Nobody got hurt. We just heard a big boom two days ago around noon. There was smoke, and then the smoke alarm went off and the sprinklers sprayed all of us. We all ran out and watched with gaping mouths as the firefighters arrived to put out the fire. Luckily, the building is fine—only the elevator is broken. Ashley thinks it was an act of terrorism; others are saying that the engine was just too old. Jack thinks it is because the engine was covered in grime and dust and wasn't cleaned properly. The building manager says the elevator shaft was hit by lightning.

"Nelly?"

"Nelly?"

"Are you there?"

Me: "Yeah!"

Ralf: "Can you believe this? You go way for two weeks and miss the most exciting thing that happened in the office since, I don't know, since ever. It was really something. We all got two days off work so that the building could be inspected before it was declared safe to be used again."

Me: "I am glad that nobody got hurt."

Tears begin to flow as soon as the phone is back on the hook. I cry for two solid hours. I don't think I have ever cried so much or so earnestly in my whole, entire life as I do today. I resolve to lay a wreath of red roses at the door of Elvi as soon as I regain my health sufficiently to be able to go back to work.

The End

It is three weeks before I feel strong enough to go back to work. Even then, I have to get a taxi to and from the office, as the physical strain of walking four flights of stairs is enough to exhaust me. When I walk into the office, both Ralf and Ashley look happy to see me.

"Nelllllllllllllllllllllllllly!" they both yell in unison, as if they greet a sport champion.

I smile in delight. I never thought I would experience a moment when I am happy to see these two. Jack comes out of his office, as well. He, too, smiles. He extends his hand in a warm handshake and says, "Welcome back!" while pulsing my limp hand up and down.

Things are slow at work. I think about my next hack job. I have the idea of creating a larger set of designs which are related but each unique. Perhaps about twenty unique images which get displayed based on a random number generator, where each time a person accesses the website, he gets a different design, making each website visit a unique experience. In place of a hand-drawn graphic, I am envisioning hand-embroidered, square pieces of canvas that are cross-stitched with a tree of life motif. Each piece shows a tree in various stages of growth and bloom, and with different birds and other animals perched on its branches. This project is the most challenging that I have done so far.

It is five whole weeks before I regain my full physical energy and go back to feeling like myself. I feel so happy to be healthy and strong again. Jack calls me to his office to tell me that Tenco has hired a batch of new employees and the CEO has asked if I would be willing to fly over and train all the new hires on our software. "There was much high praise for the job you did last time," Jack states while looking me in the eye.

"I don't know ... I am not the best candidate. You should send Ashley or Ralf, instead. They understand the app much better than I do."

"Do you know what your problem is?" asks Jack, still looking straight at me. "Your problem is that you don't realize how smart you are. You think that you are average, and then you assume that everybody around you is stupid."

"Okay, fine. I will go to Seattle," is my immediate reply.

The next week, I find myself in Seattle visiting the Tenco office. I am directed towards the meeting room that is set up for the week-long training session. After half an hour of preparation, I am greeted by seven eager trainees who look happy to see me.

At around twelve o'clock, we stop for a scheduled lunch break. At this point, the CEO walks in and greets me warmly. He shakes my hand eagerly and invites me to have lunch with him at a nearby restaurant. We go to a sushi place, where the CEO proceeds to order for both of us.

Bite-sized chunks of food arrive on two wooden trays, each bit looking colorful and delectable. My curiosity is piqued. The CEO is handling two wooden sticks as eating utensils, and I watch with amazement at his speedy dexterity with the unusual implements. When he notices that I am not eating, he asks me if I know how to use "chopsticks."

"Is that what you call these things? 'Chopsticks'?" I reply.

"No worries—I will get you a fork." He gestures to our waitress, and a fork magically appears at my side.

Me: "Is this raw fish rolled in rice?"

CEO: "Yes—sorry, I didn't realize you have never had sushi before!"

Me: "It is good to try new things."

CEO: "It is a strange concept, raw fish. But once you try it, you will be amazed at why you ever thought that cooking fish would be a good idea."

The CEO talks about how happy everybody has been with my work at Tenco, and then he proceeds to talk about his many accomplishments at work and in life. His non-stop discourse allows me to completely ignore him and focus on the myriad of tastes and textures in front of me. It looks great. The idea of serving food in compact packages suitable for a single placement in the mouth strikes me as a work of genius.

On the second day, I am taken to lunch by the COO, who treats me to an experience at a Thai restaurant.

On the third day, I am taken to lunch by the CTO, who treats me to a French restaurant.

On the fourth day, nobody shows up at noon to take me to lunch, and so I ask the receptionist to show me to Blair's office. She gestures with her hand: "Straight ahead, third office on the right."

I walk down the hallway in confident strides and knock on the door. "Come in!" I hear Blair's voice booming through the door.

He looks surprised when I walk through. There are boxes on the floor; he looks like he is moving offices.

"Hello," I say.

"Hello," says Blair.

"What is all this?" I point at the open boxes.

"I am moving to a bigger office just down the hall."

"Would you like to come grab some lunch with me? I already know three good restaurants in the area."

"No, thank you," he replies curtly.

"What is wrong? You seem annoyed."

"I sent you a letter about two months ago—no reply, nothing—not even an email."

"I am sorry about that ... I was sick."

"Sick in the head or in the heart?"

"No .. I had serious health problems."

"Aha!" He sounds skeptical.

"What do you want from me?" Now I am annoyed.

"I want you to climb on that stool and pick up those cardboard boxes on top of that shelf and place them on the floor while I enjoy watching you." He stares like a glacial mountain—ice cold and direct.

Oh! So that what this is all about. He wants to have a nice look at my bottom—a shallow reduction to a sex object. He can't handle being around an intelligent woman whose being doesn't revolve around stroking his fragile male ego. He is no different than Ashley or Ralf back in Washington—unable to handle being around a woman who is capable of independent thought. It is my fault for considering a potential for intellectual exchange and friendship.

And then the strangest thing happens. I imagine myself standing on the footstool in Blair's office, gently dragging back one of the cardboard boxes, holding it in my hands, stepping off the stool and bending down slowly to place the box on the floor, all the while feeling Blair's gaze on my behind.

A warm feeling erupts inside my abdomen. It is both disturbing and pleasurable. I feel lava pour down into my crotch. A wetness in my underwear.

That is when I remember: I am 29 years old and still a virgin.

Darn! This story is not supposed to end like this.

I give up.

I wish to thank the following people:

My son Yusuf for suggesting the title of the novel.
My family: Malik, Alexandra, Marwan, Rawan,Yarra and Yusuf for your patience with me during the process.
My editor JoJo Zawawi, for providing a steady hand.
My flamenco dance teacher, Kasandra "La China", for providing early feedback which altered the course of the novel.
My friends Rod Malkin and Franaz Ohadi for reading an early draft of the first three chapters and setting me straight.
Daryl Richter for encouraging me when I didn't believe in myself.
Barry Jakel for enocourging me when I wanted the encourgement.

Thank you!
Thank you!
Thank you!

I am dripping with gratitude.

Bruce County Public Library
1243 Mackenzie Rd.
Port Elgin ON N0H 2C6

Made in the USA
Charleston, SC
05 January 2014